"I'll tell you everything—names, dates, every-thing, but you gotta—"

"Everything about what?" Jessica cut in.

Prinzoni was white-lipped and shaking. "About the cartel."

Jessie stared at him, her eyes going cold and sav-age. The cartel. It had been her father's implacable enemy. When Jessie was still a little girl, the cartel had murdered her mother. Her father, Alex, deeply aggrieved, had repaid the killers in kind, but behind them he soon found others, and still others . . . Like a gigantic, virulent octopus, this international conspir-acy spread its tentacles of graft and corruption, its ultimate aim being to seize control of the economy of the emerging United States.

WESLEY ELLIS

LONE STAR

AND THE
HANGROPE HERITAGE

A JOVE BOOK

LONE STAR AND THE HANGROPE HERITAGE

A Jove book / published by arrangement with
the author

PRINTING HISTORY
Jove edition/July 1984

ISBN: 0-515-07734-8

Jove books are published by The Berkley Publishing Group,
200 Madison Avenue, New York, N.Y. 10016. The words
"A JOVE BOOK" and the "J" with sunburst are trademarks
belonging to Jove Publications, Inc.

PRINTED IN THE UNITED STATES OF AMERICA

★

Chapter 1

Until their return to the hotel room, the day had gone well.

Visits to San Francisco usually went well. Jessie and Ki enjoyed the young city's vigor and budding sophistication. From its initial growth explosion during the Gold Rush, San Francisco kept expanding as it became the mining capital for the Northwest and Nevada, and it was now entering a gilded age of incredible mansions on Nob Hill, and more culturally circumspect attractions than the bawdier lures of the Barbary Coast. San Francisco was acquiring a love of pomp and pleasure.

Capitalizing on this trend, Jessie spent much of the day at Gump's, arranging to supply the famous store with imported Oriental paintings, sculptures, and bronzes. She herself didn't have to, of course; as sole heiress to the worldwide Starbuck business empire, she had an army of executives and representatives to negotiate for her. But like her late father, Alex Starbuck, Jessie relished the business game—the challenge of sharp trading and the risks of high finance.

She also appreciated the posh comfort of her third-floor suite at the Lick House, preferring its traditional elegance over the much newer and more grandiose Palace Hotel. Upon entering the lobby, Jessie and Ki were greeted warmly by the manager—a deferential reception accorded the cream of the frontier's aristocracy who stayed at the Lick. As well, many of those who happened to be in the lobby just then gave the pair acknowledging nods and smiles, or, if they weren't acquainted, took discreet second glances.

"Lovely," one man murmured to Ki in passing.

Ki didn't respond. It was obvious to any man with eyes that Jessie was more than lovely; she was superbly beautiful. She was dressed just right for the occasion, in a stylish, light wool Mediterranean-blue walking suit and leghorn hat, a seal plush cape to ward off the fog, and a crook-handled India silk parasol. Her clothing was of a tailor-made fit that effectively, if modestly, displayed her full-breasted, taut-thighed figure; and her hat perched at a jaunty angle atop the soft coils of her long coppery blond hair. In the healthy bloom of her mid-twenties, Jessie had a cameo face with a pert nose and more than a hint of feline audacity to her wide-set green eyes. And there was a fluid grace about her, a freedom of movement that drew the admiration of men and the envy of women.

Conversely, ladies were apt to admire—and males to envy—Ki. A lean-featured man with bronze skin, straight blue-black hair, and almond eyes, Ki exuded a magnetic quality that suggested strong friendship when earned, and unstoppable ferocity when provoked.

Orphaned as a boy in Japan, Ki had trained in martial arts and the other skills of a samurai. Though he packed no firearm, the waistcoat and pockets of his traveling suit carried short daggers and other small throwing weapons, including the razor-sharp, star-shaped steel disks known as *shuriken*. When he'd first come to America, he'd placed his talents in the service of Alex Starbuck, Jessie's father—indeed, Ki and Jessie had virtually grown up together, and after her father's murder, it seemed only fitting for him and Jessie to continue together, as affectionate and trusting as any blood-related brother and sister could be. They were a formidable team.

A couple of bellhops took the armloads of packages from Jessie and Ki, and led the way upstairs to their adjoining suites. Jessie, true to her fashion, had celebrated her successful negotiations with Gump's by a shopping spree at Ville de Paris, where, much to Ki's discomfort, she'd studiously selected a mountain of gauzy unmentionables and assorted silken fripperies from France.

So the day had gone well, and now it was that vague hour between late afternoon and early evening. The bellhops, stacking Jessica's packages in her suite, left with a generous tip. "Dinner's next, Ki," she said, closing the door with the tip of her parasol. "Where would you like to go afterwards? The Metropolitan, or Maguire's Opera House?"

"Neither one," Ki replied, glancing at the gas jets. The room was dark, the jets unlit, and the drapes pulled, although the window behind the drapes was evidently open, judging from the raucous sounds rising from the street. "I refuse to listen to hours of fat people caterwauling."

"Be reasonable. I can't go without an escort."

"I am being reasonable. You shanghaied me once today, into accompanying you around that female shop. And what are you planning to do with it all? You don't even wear flounce-and-frill sorts of things."

"Well, just how would you know?"

Ki figured he'd best leave that one alone, and moved across to light the wall-mounted gas jets to either side of the drapes. Abruptly he stiffened—as a hand thrust

3

out from between the drapes, leveling at his chest a short-barreled pistol.

Jessie gasped and started rushing closer to help. Ki waved her to stop. She slowed, but didn't stop until she was angled close enough to be within striking distance.

"Don't try nothin'. I don't want no trouble," the hidden gunman said, his voice quavery. "I'm already *in* trouble."

"You're a bit early in the evening for larceny, sir," Jessie retorted in a cool and biting tone that bespoke hard self-control. "If you'll simply fade away, there won't have to be any trouble. And we'll consider this incident closed, if not entirely forgotten."

"I ain't here for burglarizin', lady. I'm wantin' a confab with Miss Starbuck. I've heard tell she's the only one worth coming to."

"You're talking to her," Jessie replied. "Ki, would you please fetch that lamp off the dresser there?"

There was no sound as Ki backed from the drapes and went to the dome-shaped reading lamp. The match he struck flared and sputtered, then the flame settled to a steady glow as he raised the chimney and touched the match tip to the wick. He brought the lamp over and set it on a nearby table; then, following Jessie's cue, he said trenchantly, "Okay, come on out and let's talk."

"Forget it. I'm up to be killed. There's a price on my head."

"Then take a good look at us, because we're the only ones here for you to see," Jessie said, edging nearer until she too stood in the glow of the lamp. "Might be a good idea for you to know me if you see me again. How am I to help you out of any trouble, when I don't know who you are or what you look like?"

"Aw, Christ." There was another long moment of silence, then a slight rustle of draperies, and the gunman eased into the room.

4

Jessie appraised him with steady scrutiny. She saw a nervous man in his late forties, with heavy black brows, twitchy eyes, a flat nose, a thick-lipped mouth, and a slack jaw covered with dark stubble. Under the rolled rim of a woolen cap, his black hair sprouted bushy, greasy. His clothes and flat-heeled brogans were cheap towner's garb, rumpled and stained, and a small twisted mustache indicated his vanity. He had, she thought, all the earmarks of a petty thief, a lazy braggart of a penny-ante hoodlum, and a quick-trigger backshooter.

"Now that I know what you look like," she said with more enthusiasm than she felt, "how about telling me who you are?"

Reluctantly he muttered, "Prinzoni. Willard Prinzoni."

"Fine, Will. Now how about putting away your pistol?"

"Oh no, oh no." Prinzoni backed a pace, into the draperies, waving the revolver erratically between Jessica and Ki. "I'm marked, I tell you. I've gotta get away, and you gotta help me. I know things, plenty of things, things you'll want to know, but you gotta help me get away. Till then, I ain't trustin' nobody nohow."

Ki said, "We can't help you with a gun at our heads."

"Give me sass, squinty, and I'll trade you a bullet."

Jessie realized that the gunman was truly panicked, and could crack without warning. "Easy, Will. Tell us who's after you."

Prinzoni shuffled uneasily. "I—I'll show you," he said, and shifting the pistol to his left hand, he groped with his right inside his jacket. Jessie and Ki watched closely, tensing, Ki's fingers touching his waistcoat, Jessie's grip tight on her parasol.

After fumbling in his shirt pocket, Prinzoni produced what appeared to be a torn segment of an old sepia photograph. It slipped from his quivering grasp,

5

and he bent, distracted, to retrieve it.

And Jessie swung into action. Her parasol whistled, its carved handle hooking around Prinzoni's neck, throttling the startled curse that he uttered. With a violent twist, Jessica wrenched back and aside on the parasol. Prinzoni's head snapped, his neck creaked, and his pistol flipped out of his hand while he crashed on his back on the floor, making strangled noises in his throat, his face turning a mottled greenish hue. Jessie yanked the parasol free, preparing to lambast him with its heavy handle, as the frantic gunman rolled and began to scuttle, wheezing and gagging, toward the draperies.

Ki pounced, narrowly avoiding the parasol as it cleaved air. Swiftly he curled his right arm around Prinzoni's injured throat and pulled back, drawing the hard bone of his forearm into the gunman's larynx, still keeping him on his knees, but bending his head back. In less than a second, Ki had his left arm under Prinzoni's left armpit, pushing hard against the right side of his head. Prinzoni could only make high rasping hisses like those of a throttled bird, his face changing from green to red, eyes bulging, hands clutching Ki's arm.

Ki kept him in that choke-hold until Jessica had picked up the gun and photograph. Then he released Prinzoni and straightened, watching with Jessie as the man lay shuddering, sucking in air.

Finally Prinzoni turned over, coughing. "You play rough—"

"You're lucky we didn't play for keeps," Jessie snapped, and handed the picture to Ki. "Why, I imagine we're almost as deadly as the brutal killer in your photo."

Ki smiled, understanding Jessie's sarcasm as he studied the picture. It showed an awkward, skinny little girl of twelve or so, in a faded print dress, with freckles, pigtails, and round, soulful eyes. According to a partial number and signature on the back, it was taken by one Ozgood Thorian, Portraitist, in Lake's Crossing, Nevada. Apparently this was a portion ripped from some larger family grouping, there being a little bit of a woman's skirt by the place where it had been torn, and a woman's arm about the girl's shoulder.

"Take my word for it," Prinzoni croaked, swallowing painfully. "I'll tell you everything—names, dates, everything, but you gotta—"

"Everything about what?" Jessica cut in. "About *her?*"

Prinzoni was white-lipped and shaking. "About the cartel."

Jessie stared at him, her eyes going cold and savage. The cartel. It had been her father's implacable enemy, from way back when he'd been a struggling young entrepreneur in the Orient. He'd run afoul of the cartel's greedy, coldblooded minions early on, and had fought them with all the resources at his command. When Jessie was still a little girl, the cartel had murdered her mother. Alex, deeply aggrieved, had repaid her killers in kind, but behind them he soon found others, and still others behind *them*—and even after he'd become immensely wealthy and powerful, he'd never been able to completely wipe out the cartel. Like a gigantic, virulent octopus, this international conspiracy, headed by rich and ruthless Europeans who trafficked in drugs, slavery, and prostitution, spread its tentacles of graft and corruption, its ultimate aim being to seize control of the economy of the emerging United States.

Eventually one of those tentacles managed to assassinate Alex Starbuck himself. By then, though, his daughter was old enough, and mature enough, to take his place. Jessie had his strength and cunning, along with her mother's beauty and wit. She pledged to use the Starbuck fortune and influence to continue her father's battle until the entire cartel was utterly destroyed.

And now, groveling on the carpet before her, this

fear-crazed thug was babbling that he knew names, dates, everything about the cartel. Well, he might know something. On the other hand, Prinzoni was also claiming that a scrawny twelve-year-old would be the death of him.

"Who are you, Will?" Jessie demanded sharply. "What are you to the cartel? I can't believe you know much."

"Yeah, sure, I don't look like much no more. But I used to ride with some top dogs, Sam Bass and the Youngers and suchlike, and from them I got into some pretty big stuff, mainly in Nevada."

"In Lake's Crossing, maybe?" Ki asked.

"Naw, not so much there." Prinzoni staggered upright, took a swipe at the photograph as Ki gave it back to Jessie, then stood swaying, blinking with watery eyes. "Okay, so I fell on hard times. But I tell you, that picture is your key, and it's my goddamn ticket out."

"Never mind the girl for right now," Jessie said. "What did you do that the cartel is after you?"

Prinzoni rubbed his throat, and in that moment Ki thought he heard a slight noise out in the hall. But when he focused his hearing, the sound wasn't repeated. Distant noises carried through the open window—the rattle of horses' hooves, the jingle of cable car bells, the drunken yelling of some passersby—and Ki figured he must have been mistaken.

Then Prinzoni began blurting hysterically, "Gimme back my gun! I've gotta have it, it's my only weapon, I'm nekkid without it!"

"What did you do?" Jessie insisted. "We'll stand by you, Will, but what did you do?"

"Nothin', I swear!" Prinzoni wailed. "There was a foul-up on an ol' job, and a wrong idea got spread that I was double-crossin', but I never! I never welshed! Sure, I held out about the kid, but I—"

There was a light click against glass. Ki heard it and looked up, his gaze locking on the closed transom

8

above the hall door. The barrel of a Colt .45 smashed the transom window, spraying the room with shattered glass as it hastily beat aside the remnants of the broken window. Its black muzzle arced downward, targeting—

Already Ki was in motion, reacting instinctively. He dove, knocking the lamp off the table, and tackled Jessie, sending them both tumbling to the carpet. The lamp dropped, breaking its dome and chimney, and its flame died, only to flicker obstinately. The room dimmed just as the Colt's thunderous discharge shook the walls. Black smoke curled about the transom. An errant draft from the transom reached the lamp, blowing out its meager flame. The room went entirely dark, and the gunman behind the transom swore.

Twisting around, Jessie responded with Prinzoni's stubby pistol, while the Colt blasted down at them with triphammer blasts. She emptied the cylinder at the muzzle flashes and into the door, ignoring the four staccato bursts of annihilation that raked the room, smashing furniture, punching holes in the walls, drilling into the floor. Faintly, above the earsplitting eruptions, Ki heard Prinzoni grunt with pain, and there was the dull thump of a body hitting the floor.

As quickly as the attack had begun, it was over. Running footsteps died away in the corridor, and while Jessie struck a match, Ki sprang for the door.

The hallway was pitch-dark now, someone having extinguished the gas jets. Ki plunged down its length—and tripped over the chair on which the attacker had stood. Pursuit was useless, he realized. And voices could be heard downstairs in the hotel now. Ki returned to the room, where Jessie had relighted the broken lamp and was bending over the fallen Prinzoni.

A huge red stain was spreading swiftly on Prinzoni's left breast. His eyes were closed, but momentarily they opened as he gasped, "A big help you were." Then they shut again and he died.

The voices downstairs were growing louder. Whirling, Jessie eased the door closed and said, "Hurry, we've only got a minute. See what's in his pockets."

Ki searched the body, but found nothing of significance. Jessie was neither surprised nor disappointed. "He died as he'd lived, small-time and not greatly missed," she commented, throwing a blanket over him. "I'm stumped, though, why he said the photograph is our key."

"Maybe it would make sense if we had all of the picture," Ki suggested. "The photographer's file number on the back might lead us to the original plate— assuming we can find Ozgood Thorian and Lake's Crossing."

"Lake's Crossing... somehow it seems familiar." Abruptly she smiled, snapping her fingers. "Of course! About 1868, the name for Lake's Crossing was changed to Reno." Almost as quickly she frowned, hearing steps pounding on the staircase, and after a second's consideration she asked, "Doesn't the Central Pacific have a night train heading east?"

Ki nodded. "Silver Palace sleepers, out of Oakland."

He didn't have to ask Jessie what was in her mind, or why. He knew intuitively. In a few seconds the room would be clogged with people. People with questions. Then police with questions. It would be senseless to explain about the cartel, and about Prinzoni's real reasons for being here and dying. They wouldn't be believed; they'd only be delayed, perhaps detained, for no good purpose. It would be better to mislead the police into thinking it was a simple robbery attempt, with a resultant gun fray, one robber shooting the other robber accidentally before fleeing. That would be believed, for San Francisco was a dumping ground for thieves and cutthroats.

Nor would it be sensible to stay in San Francisco. More than likely, the murderer was no higher on the criminal scale than Prinzoni had been, and was merely earning his blood money. He'd be almost impossible to catch, and scarcely worth the effort. Besides, when the cartel eventually learned that Jessie and Ki weren't dead as well, it might worry about what Prinzoni had blabbed, and decide to mount a professional attempt on their lives. Sticking around San Francisco, in that case, would be like hanging around a lion's den at feeding time.

But Prinzoni had been willing to talk in return for Starbuck protection. The cartel had shut him up while in Jessie's company, and if for no other reason, that decided her that Prinzoni's death would not be in vain. That meant tracing the photo, which meant going to Reno, which meant taking the train.

Just as the hotel manager and most of his staff lunged into the room, inundating them with questions, Ki saw Jessie glance at the corpse, and heard her speak in a low, adamant voice: "I made a deal with you, Willard Prinzoni. I aim to follow it through."

Chapter 2

Four hours later, Jessie and Ki arrived in Oakland.

The investigation had proved to be simple, the police readily accepting their version, and dismissing Prinzoni as one less lowlife to reckon with. But because it involved a Starbuck—*the* Starbuck, at that—the police had to make a performance out of routine procedures. And the idea that crooks were preying on the hotel put an onus on the manager. He kept apologizing, begging Jessie not to sue or cause a scandal. So, what with all that, packing, and buying tickets at the San Francisco terminal for the only two remaining train compartments, they'd barely made the ferry on time—and it was the last boat across the Bay before the Central Pacific's crack *Route of the Forty-niner* left on its transcontinental journey.

Leaving the ferry at its Oakland slip, they followed their porter with his wagonload of luggage, flowing with the crowd toward the train. Around them jostled laborers and farmers in work garb or mail-order clothes,

political and business moguls in broadcloth and
stovepipe hats, doll-faced ladies in hoops and crino-
line, and stout matrons dragging sleepy children. Jessie glided along with serene, almost regal indifference
to the swirl, but Ki kept trying to look everywhere at
once, feeling the weight of the hotel room gunfight
pressing in on him. He constantly wondered if the
cartel was aware of, or alarmed by, the fact that Prinzoni had been visiting them when he was gunned
down. If so, danger lurked here, danger that might
materialize at any moment.

The slip was like a long, vaulted pavilion built out
on a massive pier, open to docks at one end and tracks
at the other, and sided by cafés, shops, kiosks, and
sheds. The train's string of passenger cars was parked
flanking some of the shops, with its balloon-funneled
locomotive venting steam up ahead—pointing east.
Behind the engine and tender were mail and baggage
cars, three day coaches, the diner, and a combination
of three Silver Palace sleepers—the CP's competitor
to the Pullman—and a newfangled Mann Boudoir car,
which had exclusive compartments and prices to match.

The porter stopped by the Mann Boudoir car, and
they waited while he trundled their luggage aboard.
Facing the car was a one-chair barbershop, a faded
striped pole leaning next to its doorway. At its base
sprawled an old hound dog, asleep, its head between
its paws.

Considering the bedlam, it would have been easy
for Ki to miss what was occurring just beyond the
barbershop, but he didn't.

A young woman about Jessica's age was breath-
lessly wrestling with a worn rattan suitcase and an
oversized hatbox. That she was too poor to hire a
porter was evident in the condition of her luggage and
clothes. She wore a frayed cloth coat that draped unbuttoned, showing how tight her cheap Sicilian cloth
dress clung around her breasts and hips. Under the

13

floppy straw brim of her hat could be seen a firm profile, angry dark eyes, flushed cheeks, and a mouth, now pursed with effort, that had definitely been designed for kissing.

Or so, apparently, thought the two men badgering her. The bigger man was clad in a cutaway coat, but the quality of it reflected more taste for sport than for hard work. He was a grinner, his smile brash and perpetual, never varying. The small man had a thin, pale face and unwinking eyes that never rose above the girl's waistline. He was leaning against a makeshift guard rail that ran along the outside edge of the platform deck; behind him a short section of the slip had been torn away for rebuilding, including the floorboards and the back wall, and the guard rail was all that was saving him from a nasty spill.

"We're heading back into town for a drink," the big man was saying to the girl. "C'mon, sweets, you can catch the next train."

"I'm not going anywhere with you, so stop it."

"Don't you trust us? Hell, you'll be safe."

"I wouldn't be safe from you if I joined a convent!"

"They wouldn't let ya, sweets." The big man kept grinning, but his lips curled. "Don't act snooty with us. We know what you are."

The girl plunked down her suitcase and hatbox, then stalked over and swung a roundhouse slap at the man's face. With startling quickness he caught her wrist before she struck him and gave it a twist, imprisoning her. The girl bit his arm and began kicking his shins.

Ki frowned. He was reluctant to interfere, because it could attract attention to him and Jessie, right at a time when they daren't risk any. Yet the two men didn't appear willing to let the girl alone and go about their business, without some stiff persuasion.

"Let go!" the girl shouted angrily.

The barber glanced out of his shop, a shaving brush full of lather in his hand, mild curiosity on his face.

His dog raised its sleepy head and stared mournfully at the men and the girl, then sank down wearily again. The men ignored the barber and the dog, the small man still staring at the girl's crotch, while the big man pulled her closer and started talking to her in low, hungry tones.

"Get on board," Ki said to Jessie, and sprang across to the barbershop. He snagged the shaving brush from the barber's grasp, sloshed it across the hound's muzzle, and tossed the brush back.

"Mad dog!" he yelled, sprinting toward the men and the girl.

"What?" The big man shoved the girl aside and pivoted. Ki's shoulder caught him halfway around, butting him back against the guard rail, which splintered under his weight. He teetered above the hole in the flooring, arms windmilling, trying to find the small man, who was leaning in an attempt to grab him.

"Hold on!" Ki encouraged, pushing the small man. Then he jumped back from the edge, seizing the girl in his arms to keep her from falling, while the two men plummeted, howling, limbs gyrating, to splat into the dank mud flat beneath the slip.

Ki set the girl down by her luggage, forgetting to take his arms away as he glanced at the barbershop. The barber hadn't moved and neither had his hound, which was still lying at the base of the pole, lethargically licking the lather off its chops.

Chuckling, Ki released the girl, who promptly slapped his cheek. From the vestibule of the car, Jessie let out a big laugh. Ki, one hand on his cheek, turned and gave her a sour look; still laughing, Jessie disappeared into the car. Then Ki eyed the girl ruefully.

"Well, somebody was deserving of a slap," she declared irately, and then, as if realizing the absurdity of her remark, she smiled hesitantly. "I'm sorry, I was upset, is all. I am grateful."

At the tail of the train, the conductor sounded his departure call. The girl shrugged as Ki picked up her luggage, and she started forward along the train, until Ki caught her arm and reversed her.

"I'm riding coach," she explained, moving to continue.

"Not this trip," he said.

She pulled her arm, but Ki's grip remained secure. She shrugged again and walked with him back along the train, as the engineer began to ease into his couplings, one by one. When Ki halted by his car, she glanced up. "How much do you figure this will cost me?"

"Nothing. Not even gratitude."

"That's what they all say," she murmured as he handed her up the steps, following her with an easy swing of his body.

The Mann Boudoir car had two washrooms, polished wood paneling, real sheets, its own conductor, and—best of all—locked-door privacy. Ki handed his ticket to the conductor, saying, "This is for her. I didn't have time to buy one at the station." The conductor nodded, grinning when he saw the bank note tucked in with the ticket.

As they went on down the corridor, the girl said, "You didn't have to do that, you know."

"No, I didn't have to. Let's leave it at that."

She nodded quietly. When they were finally alone in his compartment, she didn't sit down, but stood gazing around. "Say, this is high-tone. What am I doing here?"

"What are any of us doing here?" Ki responded, and while he thrust her suitcase up on the rack, where the porter had already placed his bag, he introduced himself. She told him her name was Francine, Mrs. Francine MacNear. Her eyes had seen a lot, and her blond hair was probably dyed, but with her coat off, her figure was stunning.

"I should be back home in Elrod, South Dakota, that's where. No, I shouldn't," Francine continued, opening her hatbox and removing a fifth of whiskey.

16

She kept the bottle while Ki added her hatbox to the rack and found some glasses. "I ought to remember I was a sweet, happy li'l innocent, but I wasn't. I've never been. But, oh, what am I doing here—or going to be doing in Virginia City?"

"Is your husband in Virginia City?" Ki asked as he poured.

"No. A new job, at the Silverado." She took off her shoes and they sat on the bunk together. "I was working in San Francisco. My husband is, uh, in jail there." Her slim leg pressed against Ki's thigh as she tilted her glass, sipping. "God, that's vile."

"A shame. About your husband, I mean," Ki temporized. "I'd think a man would want to keep his nose clean, with a fine wife like you."

Tears misted in Francine's eyes. "I'm not very fine, Ki, but thanks anyway." She curled up beside him, and he ran the tips of his fingers along her back. She was warm, and squirmed under his caress. "Ki. I don't even know your whole name, and here I sit comfy on your bed, in need of another drink."

Ki poured a refill. Gently she wriggled free and rose, wandering to the center of the swaying compartment with her glass in hand. She surveyed him, smiling faintly, the light from the bracket lamp gleaming from the shiny, lush-looking curves of her dress. Ki said after a while, "Stop staring at me."

"I'm not staring."

"Well, whatever you're doing, do something else."

"All right." With one hand she unbuttoned her dress and expertly peeled it up her voluptuous body, somehow getting it off over her head without losing a drop of her drink. All she wore now were stockings and lace-edged drawers and a corset that didn't do much except to accentuate the lower curve of her breasts.

"What are you, Ki? What are you, truly?"

Ki leaned forward, watching, his blood pumping faster. Her free hand undid the corset and slid it off. It lay on the floor, and his eyes moved from it to her

17

stockings, up to where she was untying the drawstring of her drawers. He began removing his boots.

"I know what I am," Francine said when Ki failed to answer. "I'm a soldier, I think, that's what I am." Creamy flesh appeared at her hip as she slowly slipped the drawers down her thighs. She stepped out of them, but didn't bother to remove her gartered brown stockings. Their shade, a deep cinnamon, matched the rich color of her pubic mound. "Yes sir, I'm the best trooper in the world."

Standing, Ki shed his jacket and shirt, and was almost free of his pants when she murmured, "The *best*. But you're going to conquer me. Lord, you're going to bloody well gut me with that sword."

She licked her lips, as though anticipating her sweet surrender, then crossed to the bunk and stretched out, putting her glass down on the floor. He moved close, staring down at her flesh and silk, cream and brown, preparing to delve between her wide-splayed thighs.

But Francine was faster, greedier. She turned slightly, raising herself on one elbow, and kissed his protruding erection. She nipped it with her tongue and sucked its fleshy length into her mouth, clinging to his thighs, hiding her head shyly in the shadows of his groin, while his aching maleness swelled between her lips. She curved her fingers around his hips, forcing him deeper, pinioning his girth down into her throat, her brazenly bobbing motion quickening until she fell away from him, unexpectedly releasing him from her mouth when he least desired freedom.

"In me, now," she whispered. "Do me, damn you, do me in."

Ki mounted her as she spread herself, wide and welcoming, for his assault. He plunged into her, and she pressed her loins up against him, her legs crossing above his buttocks and locking him into the gripping cradle between her thighs. His body pounded hers against the thin mattress, and they rolled crazily with the swing of the car.

18

A train berth is not the ideal spot, Ki thought dizzily, for such frenzied sport. But that was about all he thought, as they panted in concentration, pummeling each other with ever-quickening strokes.

Ki pumped into her until she was a hot river, until he could feel her not knowing or caring who or what that thing inside her was, just driving it up and down inside her with lavish fanaticism.

"Don't stop, not yet!" she pleaded loudly, even while he felt her inner sheath contracting spasmodically from her erupting orgasm. The locomotive whistle wailed into the night, with Francine wailing as well—and Ki climaxed with her, spurting deep inside her. And long after they were both good for nothing, Francine was still shrieking, "Don't stop!"

"Enough," Ki said. "Whoever's in the next compartment will think I'm beating you."

She calmed and snuggled against him, damp with sweat, her long fingers entwined with his. "Again, in a while," she sighed, and fell asleep. Ki lay beside her, passing the time in meditation.

Some while later the locomotive whistled again, and the car began rocking over unballasted roadbed, its pony trucks rattling through a series of switch points. There was a sudden cutting off of the throbbing exhaust, replaced by the quivering roar of the engine blower and the clanging peal of the bell as the train shuddered to a halt. Lights glowed vaguely beyond the compartment's drawn window shade, and voices could be heard trackside. They'd stopped in Sacramento, Ki realized, where the train would cut onto the mainline east.

Francine slumbered soundly through the disturbance. Shortly the bell clanged, and the car lurched, beginning to move out of the depot. The train clattered on its unhurried way toward the Sierra peaks, its trucks beating a lulling rhythm as they clicked over rail joints.

Ki half-dozed himself, for a while, then his eyes snapped open. He thought he'd heard something, a faint cry. He looked at Francine, but she was still placidly dead to the world, so he eased away from her and peaked out under the shade. They were somewhere in the mountains, still climbing. Darkness was thick against the forested slopes and valleys, with the moon clouded over.

He stood for a moment, perplexed, edgy.

Then came the scream. It wasn't one of terror or despair; it was a blistering, high-pitched cry of alarm. And he knew whose it was.

"Jessie!"

She had retired, alone, about the same time Ki was testing out his berth with Francine. Preparing for bed, she had changed into a floor-length gown of pink-striped domet flannel, brushed out her hair and re-pinned it so she could sleep on it, and extinguished the bracket lamp. She was so tired that she was barely conscious of the stop at Sacramento, and dropped off again immediately afterwards.

She was awakened by the man closing her compartment door.

The click of the latch was very gentle, but it was sufficient to alert her. The man had probably picked the lock, she thought; but however he had sneaked in, he *was* in, and nervous. She could hear the shallow unevenness of his breathing, and judged that he was no more than three feet away. And she had her back to him, with her only way out blocked, and no way to call for help or defend herself before he could reach her and strike. Her only slim chance lay in his skittishness.

Feigning sleep, she slowly turned over and, as she'd hoped, her motion stalled him. He froze for a good half-minute before he moved again, allowing Jessie time to peek covertly at him.

The compartment was dark, but a softer darkness than the hard black of his silhouette. He was short, quite stocky, and hatless, and he wore the loose-fitting shirt and pants of a Mexican peon. He had a skinning knife in his right hand, and pointed its long thin blade at her as he gingerly tested the floor. His sandals made no sound as he tiptoed closer.

Sweat prickled Jessie's neck. A foolish move would kill her, but so might no move at all. Cautiously the man crept within two feet of the berth, then a floorboard creaked warningly. He drew back, wanting to think about it awhile before risking another step.

That was when Jessie threw herself sideways out of the berth, kicking against the wall for leverage. She spun right out and dropped, scrambling to face him, seeing him wrench his knife out of the mattress. A difference of a second, and it would have been in her.

He sprang at her, blade up, slicing. She backed away, twisting aside. He followed, overeager in his haste to stab her and escape. Again Jessie dodged, this time pivoting an extra step, so that as he charged, she was able to club the back of his neck with her locked fists, the way Ki had taught her to do. The man stumbled, and caromed off the window. She grabbed his knife wrist and smashed it against the sharp edge of the window frame, and the knife fell to the floor.

Cursing, the man punched her in the stomach. She reeled, gasping for air, but managed to kick the knife away before he could retrieve it. His foot stamped viciously on her bare toes, his hands clamping around her throat and throttling her like a rag doll.

Struggling to keep from blacking out, Jessie countered by grabbing the man between his legs, squeezing and twisting with all her strength. The man bellowed in pain and let go. She didn't release her grip, but clutched him still harder—until, with an anguished snarl, he knocked her hand loose, hit her again, and dove for his knife.

Staggering off balance from his blow, Jessie plowed into him just as he was scooping up the knife. She went down, dragging him with her. He groaned and then they thrashed silently, tumbling together, desperate. The man finally shoved free and lunged upright, and for a moment Jessie thought it was all over for her.

But instead of attacking her, the man lurched for the door, his breath now coming in rasping grunts. He clawed open the door, and by the dim light in the corridor, Jessie saw the knife sticking out of his belly. Somehow, during their tussle, he'd inadvertently stabbed himself. Blood was gouting, spattering in an ugly trail behind him as he careened down the corridor.

Jessie got to the doorway and screamed like a banshee.

The conductor, who'd evidently been dozing on his bench beside the far washroom door, abruptly appeared at the other end of the corridor. Bravely he started forward, only to be rammed aside by Ki charging out of his compartment, naked, wrapped in a sheet.

The pain-maddened knifer had pulled out his blade, and was holding it defiantly in one hand, clutching his bleeding gut with the other. Ki glimpsed Jessica, looked relieved, then regarded the man again, just as he hurtled toward him. Letting the sheet fall, oblivious of his nudity, Ki launched himself across the short distance with a *tobi-geri* flying kick, his left foot catching the man in his wounded abdomen, buckling him backward in a heap.

But the man was either abnormally strong or insane with impending death. Still clutching his ruptured belly with his left hand, his knife seemingly glued to his right fist, he came rebounding at Ki, using that same upward stab with which he'd tried to disembowel Jessie.

Ki went at the man like a wolf leaping for the jugular, his left hand darting to clutch the knife arm, while his right lashed out to crush the man's windpipe.

The swaying car lurched violently just at the mo-

22

ment of impact, and Ki's well-aimed punch slewed under the man's jawline, spinning him half around. The car wrenched again as the tracks curved sharply onto a gorge-spanning trestle, and the man floundered against Ki, still trying to stab, more dead than alive but refusing to admit it.

Ki's arms roped about him, under his arms, holding him firmly. "Open the vestibule door," Ki ordered the conductor, ignoring the man's crazed thrashing. The conductor hesitated, unsure, fearful. "Open it!" Ki snapped, shifting his grip, reaching up to clasp hands behind the man's bull-like neck.

When Ki heard the telltale rush of wind from the vestibule, he thrust the man harshly along the corridor. The man struggled to break the hold, his arms forced up and out, his head downward at a punishing angle, as what Ki was planning for him sparked in his dying mind. "No! You can't! Give me a break!"

"I'm giving you the same break you've given others." His features as bleak as granite, Ki heaved the man up to the open vestibule door, then flung him out. He grabbed the step-rail to keep from following, and watched as the man struck the edge of the trestle's crossties, rolled, then plunged over, his fading howls echoing up from the inky black depths. Then Ki reached out and closed the door.

"Jesus Christ, mister, Jesus Christ," the conductor said. He was shivering and ashen-faced, and when he glanced down the corridor, where other passengers were now peering querulously from their compartment doors, he took out a handkerchief and mopped his brow.

"I liked it less than you did," Ki said gravely.

"Sure . . . sure. And it ain't like the feller didn't warrant it, or wasn't gonna die anyhow. But I dunno, I jus' dunno, mister. What am I going to tell my supervisor, huh? How can I explain?"

"Tell him the truth," Ki replied, walking back to

his sheet. "A sneak thief got on board, cut himself, then tried to escape and fell off the train."

"Oh, that's a pip. They'll can me for certain."

"Why? You braced him first, and without resorting to gunfire that could have struck innocent riders. You're a hero, and he's not around to contradict you, is he?" Winding the sheet about him like a Roman toga, Ki continued along the corridor to where Jessie still stood in her compartment doorway. "You're not hurt, Jessie?"

She shook her head.

"What was he after?" Ki asked.

"Me dead, nothing else." Jessie reached out and removed her name card, which the well-intentioned conductor had posted on her door, and wadded it in her fist. "I won't be so easy to find, next time," she said, then consoled, "You shouldn't feel bad, Ki. I know, your code insists that you act to spread justice and goodwill; but by the same 'doctrine of duress,' it's better to commit a crime than to let a greater evil persist. To be honest, I can't say I'm sorry."

"Still, it was a waste. He knew things."

"Maybe. But I think he'd have died before talking. With him gone, at least, we might be able to slough this off the way we did Prinzoni's death, and avoid drawing more interest in us than is necessary."

"I already mentioned something along those lines to the conductor." Ki turned, spotting the conductor down the corridor, calming some passengers. "I doubt he'll be any trouble," Ki added, regarding Jessie again. "No, our trouble will be in Reno. If that man sneaked on at Sacramento, as I suspect he must have, it means the cartel knew we were aboard."

Jessie yawned. "I just hope there's no more trouble until Reno. I'm bushed." She bade Ki good night and wearily closed her door.

When Ki returned to his compartment, he found Francine still fast asleep, apparently having been comatose throughout the entire uproar. But when he climbed in alongside her, she began to stir, her hand sliding teasingly down his body and fondling him gently. "My, wasn't that a nice nap," she murmured. "Are you all rested?"

Chapter 3

In the blush of a fiery autumnal dawn, the train paralleled the Truckee River, heading across the scrubby High Plains plateau, and rumbled to a brake-shivering halt at the Jesse E. Reno station.

Ki was one of the first to alight, reaching up his hand to assist Francine to the platform. She looked chipper, if slightly rumpled, in her same frayed outfit. Ki looked a bit haggard, but was now clad in denims, a collarless cotton-twill shirt, and moccasin-style slippers. The weapons from his suit he'd secreted in the many pockets of his worn leather vest.

Jessie waited until a few other passengers had gone ahead of her, not wishing to intrude on Ki and the girl. She too had changed into more workaday clothes, and when she stepped lithely from the vestibule, she was wearing a plain silk blouse and form-hugging jeans and jacket. A derringer was concealed behind the wide square buckle of her belt, and her custom .38 Colt was holstered at her thigh. This may not have appeared as stylish as yesterday's fashionable ensemble, but considering all that had happened, it was much more sensible.

A problem was all the luggage. Except for Ki's bag, it was hers; she could travel light, and would have, if she'd known she'd be dressing for frontier mayhem instead of refined society. So be it; her belongings had to be parked until they learned if they were staying in Reno.

She collared the station baggage clerk, a red-faced lout with ferretlike eyes. He refused to store it, stating that his room was only for paying passengers, not the general public. A winsome smile and five silver dollars changed his mind. Giving Jessie a claim check, he lumbered off in search of a dolly big enough to wrestle her luggage.

While Jessie was bribing the clerk, Ki and Francine were saying their farewells, which were mercifully brief and cheerful. Ki asked, "You're taking the Virginia & Truckee on from here, I suppose?"

"God, no, it's too much money."

Ki nodded, aware that the V&T Railroad was the most expensive short line on earth. "Well, Virginia City's a long walk."

She said, "I'll try to hitch a wagon ride, or if nobody's driving that way, I'll see if there's space in the mail car."

"Listen, you don't have—"

She silenced him with a gentle finger on his lips. "Not this trip," she said, echoing Ki's words in Oakland. "Last night was a trade-off, kinda, but anything more and I'd feel beholden to you." She picked up her suitcase and hatbox, turned, then paused to smile teasingly. "If you ever get up my way, I'll be at the Silverado."

As she hurried away, struggling with her case and box, Jessie approached Ki. He nodded, but didn't say anything for a moment, his attention still focused on

27

Francine. There was a certain restlessness to her, he thought, as though her one-night adultery with him had left a pleasant taste in her mouth, but she was now anxious to get on with her life and forget it.

Finally he said, "I'll bet you, Jessie."

"No, thanks. You know the girl, I don't."

He grinned, shaking his head. "About Ozgood Thorian. He was an itinerant photographer who chanced through Reno once, and he's never been heard of since; or he's been heard of as having died. Pick your choice."

"You lose both. Thorian's retired, living right here, as he always has. I asked the baggage clerk, and he gave me exact directions."

"They must be short, considering the size of the town," Ki remarked as they started walking along the dusty main street.

Reno was small, but boisterous and vibrant with life. Much of it was centered back at trackside, where trainmen and passengers and a mustachioed sheriff were grouped around the conductor, listening to him expound on his death-defying combat with the sneak-thief knifer. Yet there was bustling activity elsewhere, farmers and ranchers and mine laborers moving briskly on horseback or in wagons. On foot, they mingled with bonneted women along the boardwalks. The flanking shops and dwellings bloomed with lights and open doorways, despite the relatively early hour. Reno was thriving, busily tending to its business.

The trick was to catch anyone who was more interested in *their* business than in his own. Jessie and Ki kept a wary lookout. Another ambushing killer could be stalking them, but they didn't spot anything suspicious as they neared the address Jessie had been given.

Three sides of a wide square at Third and Ralston consisted of false-fronted saloons and dance halls, a gray stone bank, and a ramshackle hotel. The fourth side contained a row of peak-roofed brick-and-board

28

houses. They might have been attractive when they were first erected, but now they were past their prime.

Number 35 was still making a brave show. Flower patches bordered the front porch, and although the paint was on its last gasp, the window curtains looked bright and clean. The front door was of dark oak, with a bear's head carved in wood for a knocker. Jessie lifted the bear's head and knocked.

There was a pause, and Ki leaned against the porch rail, feeling the morning sun hot on his back. Jessie was about to knock again when they heard shuffling footsteps and the front door opened.

A tiny gnome stood in the doorway, a wizened hand resting against the doorframe. The old man had a knobby head that sported a sticking plaster over one ear, and a thick-lensed pince-nez perched on a button nose. He had on carpet slippers, butternut trousers, and a white shirt; out of the shirt's collar, his scrawny neck and head were thrust forward like a snapping turtle's.

"Howdy," he said. "What can I do you for?"

A blast of gin-soaked breath seared Jessica's face. "Mr. Thorian?"

"Yep." He sagged against the doorpost, patently drunk.

"My name is Jessica Starbuck," she said, "and this is my friend, Ki. Could we bother you for some information? It's to do with a photograph you took some years ago."

"My dear people, naturally. Come in and join me in a drink." He stood aside. "Glad to meet you. Matter of fact, I was getting bored as a tick. D'you people ever get bored?"

Jessie replied that she could not recall ever being bored.

"Lucky you." Thorian sounded as if he meant it. He ushered them into a sitting room, which was comfortable but busy with overstuffed furniture, Victorian bric-a-brac, and framed photos.

29

A woman was sitting on the sofa, sour-faced and glaring at them. She was blowsy, of indeterminate age, though Jessie suspected the face powder and paint she was wearing lowered it many years. Other than a terrycloth bathrobe, she was wearing nothing.

"Alone, Ozgood," she said, rising. "You promised."

"This is . . . Who'd you say you were?" Thorian asked, screwing up his eyes and peering at Jessie.

"Starbuck. But if we're intruding—"

"Naturally not." Thorian patted Jessie's hand. "Mabel, my child, Miss Starbuck and her companion have important affairs to discuss with me. Shall we postpone our session until tomorrow?"

Mabel glowered at him, then swiveled and stamped barefoot across to an inner doorway. Thorian wasn't watching her leave; he was already at a sideboard loaded with bottles, and, his back to her, was pouring gin into a tumbler. Mabel swept through the doorway; Thorian turned around, said, "Skoal!" and swallowed thirstily; and somewhere in the rear of the house, a door slammed violently.

"I'm sorry," Jessie began, "we didn't—"

Thorian laughed. "Nonsense. I'm tickled you came a-calling. That gal drives me balmy." He refilled his glass, sighed, and waved them to chairs. "Sit down, relax. What was it you wanted?"

Jessie took the torn picture of the little girl out of her jacket pocket and offered it to Thorian. "This is part of a portrait, we believe, that you made way back when Reno was still Lake's Crossing."

Thorian squinted at the photo, then went with it over to a window so he could see it better. "Yep, this is one of mine," he said, and glanced at the back. "Yep, here's my name, too."

"What can you tell us about it? What do you remember?"

"That sure was a fair time ago, wasn't it? Uh-huh,

30

'67 or '68, I'd hazard, when I was still making negatives by the wet-plate process. Matter of fact, this print's on albumenized paper, toned with gold—"

"No, what about who's in it?"

"The subjects? Who the devil can remember subjects?" Thorian returned the photo to Jessie and moved unsteadily to a tall cupboard from which, after some poking, he removed a big leatherbound register. He settled in the closest chair and began thumbing through the pages. "That's why I had to log 'em by my plate numbers, for them who wanted copies later. Yep, here it is: Balsam—Enoch, Adabelle, Unity; June 30, 1866; FY2C." He set the register down. "A family portrait, my yard, two prints, paid cash."

Ki asked, "Do you still have the plate?"

"Can't sell prints without keepin' negatives, can I?" He groaned as he hoisted himself out of the chair and shuffled toward the doorway through which Mabel had exited. Jessie and Ki trailed him down a hall, past the kitchen and a pantry rigged as a darkroom, and into a back bedroom that was crammed from floor to ceiling with boxes and slat crates. "It's filed in here somewhere," Thorian said, scratching his head.

They helped him hunt, Ki hauling out the cartons of exposed glass negatives, while Jessie and Thorian checked their numbers. Some plates were cracked and others were foggy and deteriorated, but most still seemed to have images of sharp, fine grain. It gave Jessie hope.

After a spell of this, Thorian took a break to get his glass of gin. When he returned and began searching again, he said, "Balsam, Enoch Balsam. It's coming back to me, a little. Handsome rogue. Billed himself as a miner, but somehow I've got the notion he didn't care for regular work. His missus was a wowser, a plumb knockout, and the kid was strapping for only bein' ten. Howdy, what's this?"

31

Grinning, he carefully handed Jessie a plate. She took it to the window, nudged the curtains aside, and held it up to the sunlight.

The negative image was backward, of course, and no good for details. Its contrasts were clear enough, though, for her to make out Enoch Balsam standing tall and stiff, clad in a baggy shirt over a pair of duck trousers that were stuffed into knee-high boots, his face mostly covered by a Bismarck beard. Seated next to him was his wife, Adabelle, petite and slender, with piquant features and curling hair, the rest of her undecipherable in a long flowing wrapper. Close beside her was the girl, Unity, her mother's arm on her shoulder, just as in the picture. Now, seeing them as a group, Jessie could discern that the daughter had inherited bigness from her father, but that facially she resembled her mother, her sad saucer eyes in particular.

She gave the plate to Ki, who, like her, handled it by its edges as he scrutinized the image. She asked Thorian, "Can you remember anything else about the Balsams, or what might've become of them?"

"Nope, haven't the faintest," Thorian answered, then paused, his brow wrinkling. "I bite my tongue, ma'am, I'm suddenly of a mind where I got my low opinion of Enoch. From the news stories, I rec'lect, of how he was a member of the gang that robbed a train outside Virginia City. Killed the express guard and got away with a lot of money in bullion, losing a posse that was hot on their hocks. All 'cept Enoch Balsam. He didn't get away—he got roped on the spot."

"You mean he was caught and hanged? He's dead?"

"Well, I hope for his sake he is. His widow cut him down and buried him proper, according to how the *Enterprise* had it writ."

Ki returned the plate. "We want a copy, if possible."

32

"Might be, might not. Printing off a negative this old can be dicey." Thorian squinted again, examining the glass. "Give me an hour to try. No, best make it two. I'll be needing lots of sun." He looked up quizzically. "Why're you interested in the Balsams?"

"We're tracing a long-lost relative named Adabelle," Ki improvised hastily, and turned to go. "Thanks. We'll be back."

"Say, that kid'd be in her twenties now, I calc'late." Thorian winked slyly. "Fresh an' firm, way her ma was. Not like Mabel, though I admit her 'Grecian nymph' poses are pop'lar items with the gents. But listen, if you bump into the kid, ask her if she'd model for me."

"Two hours, at the latest," Jessie confirmed archly. "And don't disturb yourself, Mr. Thorian. We can find our way out."

Leaving his house, she stalked to the square, eyeing Ki indignantly. "The nerve of him! Come on, we're going where it's cleaner."

"The V&T depot." It was a statement, not a question.

Jessie nodded. "Thorian's memory may be as twisted as his morals, but if he's right, the train Balsam robbed had to be a Virginia & Truckee."

Located in its own section of railyard, the V&T depot was a midget mansion of gingerbread and dormers and a flag-masted cupola. On a nearby siding, a stubby locomotive stewed quietly, linked to a half-dozen freight cars and empty coaches.

The few people in the waiting room appeared to be just waiting, which indicated that the train wasn't due to depart for quite a while. The stationmaster was sorting change behind his wicket; he was fat, with a dead cigar clamped in his teeth, and looked hot in his dark uniform.

He gazed without interest at Jessie and Ki. "Yeah?"

33

"Some time back," Jessica said, "one of your trains was robbed of a bullion shipment. Do you remember the incident?"

"Why?"

Ki grinned genially. "Ever read *Crime Fact Weekly?*"

"Never heard of it."

"It's like the *Police Gazette*, only different," Ki explained. "Our editor thought the heist would make a swell article."

"You have a job on, don't you? That was five years ago."

"Sure, but sometimes, when you start digging into ancient history, you get on better than if it just happened."

"No kidding." The stationmaster tried relighting his cigar, but gave up and said, "Well, I was a spring pup with the company then, but was working outta Virginia City, so what I know is first-hand. Boomtime, it was, not like nowadays; and it was one of the largest shipments ever, gold and silver both, mostly from the Ophir mine. The train was guarded, but not against dynamite. Twenty minutes out, the bandits blasted the engine apart, then the express car, and they threatened to blow up the other cars if there was any resistance."

"Nobody knew them?"

"They were hooded. Used burros to pack the bullion and themselves back into the hills. Believe me, they were eight slick professionals, and their only slip-up was not figuring on the marshal's nephew."

"How's that?"

"Storey County's marshal, ol' Fritz Tilden, has a part-Comanche nephew who can track better'n a coon dog. Him an' Tilden an' a bunch of townsfolk larruped off in pursuit, and cornered the bandits above Dishwater Creek. The bandits held them off for upwards of a week, then managed to slink away in the dark. With all the bullion, too. Nary hide nor hair of them

34

or the loot has turned up to this day."

Jessie frowned. "But we heard one of them was captured."

"Oh yeah, Enoch Balsam. A salty cuss, shot up so bad he couldn't talk, much less escape. Him and the burros, that's all the posse found, and by then they were so mad they lynched him out of spite. The reward's still open on the bullion, if that's your angle."

"No angles. We're just looking about and seeing what we can pick up," Ki replied amiably. "It's an interesting story. Seven men slip through a posse and vanish, along with an ore shipment that was so heavy it had required a team of burros to haul it that far. How did they do it? And where have they gone? Have you any ideas?"

"Me? Lawdogs and fortune hunters have uprooted land and scoured mines, and it's foxed them. I ain't brighter than them." The stationmaster scowled and fiddled with his cigar, obviously losing interest in the discussion. "Well, if that's all that's on your mind—"

"Not quite," Jessie said. "Two tickets, please."

"Virginia City, I wager." Taking her money, the stationmaster warned, "Train leaves promptly in an hour and twenty-seven minutes."

"That means," Jessie said to Ki as they exited the depot, "Filthy Thorian is going to see us sooner than he expects."

They returned to the Central Pacific station, where Jessie arranged for their luggage to be transferred to the Virginia & Truckee. Reno's fledgling weekly didn't date back far enough to have reported the heist, they learned, and the sheriff's office was a source they preferred not to test. So they went to a café where they could sit with their backs to the wall, facing the entrance, and ordered lunch.

It was a quick meal, and they spent it speculating upon the strange, seemingly disconnected sequence of events. A petty crook named Prinzoni, seeking sanctuary from a little girl, or maybe because of the girl, in return for information about the cartel. Or perhaps the girl had nothing to do with it, and Prinzoni was simply deluded or trying to pull a fast one. In any case, the little girl was now a big girl, assuming she was still alive—which was more than could be said for her father, whose brief career as a train robber might not have importance, either. The vanished bullion was motive for anything; but that holdup was five years old—and the torn photo was fourteen—and could have absolutely no bearing on the murderous attacks of the previous day.

There was no pattern, but only a puzzle with some pieces that may or may not fit into it. They had to work with no clear idea in mind, save that the cartel was determined to stop them from solving the puzzle.

They walked toward Thorian's house, both of them troubled in thought. When they reached the square, they stood a moment, scanning its desultory stir of traffic—men going into and coming out of the hotel across the way; others entering and leaving the saloons; a ranch rig jouncing down the street toward the river.

A tall, loose-jointed man ran out from the side of Thorian's house. Not pausing, he headed diagonally across the square, away from where they stood watching him, at a pace that was half dogtrot, half lope. Everything about him suggested frantic haste.

Giving each other an anxious glance, they sprinted for Thorian's. They were almost to the front path when the door swung open and Mabel came out. She stood motionless on the porch, her hand clutching its rail, a bright red trickle of blood flowing down her chin from the corner of her mouth. There was a patch of blood about the size of a fist on the left side of her bathrobe.

They stared up at her, Jessie's mouth turning dry. Mabel's painted face tightened, her legs went rub-

36

bery, her knees hinged, her hand slid off the rail. Then she fell, striking the porch step with her shoulder and slithering the rest of the way on her back to land on the walk.

Before they could get to her, they knew she was dead.

But they never did get to her. There was a deafening roar, a rending of wood and a rumble of cascading bricks, a cloud of yellowish smoke gushing from inside the house. Through the turmoil knifed a scream of agony, cut off short.

The eruption knocked Jessie and Ki to the ground, just a fraction of a second before shattered glass and jagged chunks of wall swept lethally overhead like scythes. The front door was hammered half off its hinges, and hung crazily until, an instant later, there was a second explosion as Thorian's photographic chemicals ignited. Timber lanced through the air. More bricks flew wildly from the shattered house. Volcanic flames streaked through the smoke.

Jessie and Ki picked themselves up slowly, choking in the thick atmosphere and brushing bits of debris from their faces and clothes. The smoke and fire began swirling in a vortex, and they could see that where the house had been, everything was now a fiery shambles. One entire side had been blown away. The blazing roof sagged on its shattered beams. Camera equipment, papers, and that archive of negatives had been scattered like leaves, and lay smashed and ruined.

The square was in a turmoil of near panic. Crowds boiled from the saloons, hotel, bank, and other homes, all shouting and gesticulating. Nobody knew at that moment what had happened, but common sense told them the house was doomed. They could only try to keep the fire from spreading to the other buildings.

The milling throng raced for water, returning one after another, soon forming a bucket brigade. Jessie and Ki joined in to help keep the buckets coming and going. A score of paces away, they spotted a portion of Thorian's mangled body, but Mabel had disappeared under the mounded rubble.

Perversely, a slight breeze cropped up from the east, fanning the flaming structure and scattering sparks that drove the crowd back. The mustachioed sheriff and a couple of deputies arrived and pitched in. Other men stamped out the flaming debris that had fallen outside the bucket brigade's ring. Then the breeze faded and everyone breathed easier, though fearful determination kept the bucket line working feverishly.

From the direction of the depot, a steam whistle blew.

"The train, Jessie," Ki called. "We can still catch it."

Nodding, Jessie eased away from the line, then hesitated, surveying the scene of fiery desolation. Yes, it was time to go, she thought; they'd done all they could, and they were finished here. The bomber who'd set the dynamite had seen to that—but he'd failed to finish their mission. He'd bungled his job, at the cost of two innocent lives. What a waste!

Ki touched her arm, beckoning. Tears welled in her eyes, but her expression was more angry than sad as they hastened toward the depot.

★

Chapter 4

They reached the depot just as the train was pulling out. Angling past the depot, they ran for the tracks and intercepted the last coach as it began to pass by. Ki hustled Jessie forward, gave her a boost to the observation deck steps, then reached for a grab-iron and swung himself aboard.

After a pause to catch their breaths, they opened the deck's glass-paneled door and stepped into rolling comfort—mahogany paneling, bright brass fittings, deep upholstery, an aisle roof high enough to clear a top hat. The coach carried a large quota of gentry, but there were a number of tinhorns and stock promoters and grubstake seekers, and quite a few just plain common folk. Or so Jessie and Ki estimated, surveying the passengers before taking an empty double seat.

The train curved southward, and soon began following the course of what appeared to be a branch of the Truckee River. It rolled across broad stretches of jagged rock and massed boulders, easing around gullies and toiling up grades covered with buckbrush, dawdling at every riverbank hamlet like a milk-run local. And as the day progressed, the arcing sun burned down on it with increasing pressure. The heat made the purpling mountains and dusty alkaline expanses dance weirdly, when viewed through the coach's blown-glass windows.

At Carson City, a freight car was unhitched for the spur line to Gardnerville. A few passengers got on and off, and peddlers came through hawking their wares, the only ones enjoying the long delay.

From there the train meandered eastward, threading the southeastern foothills of the Ruby Mountains in the early-afternoon glare. Behind to the west fell the serrated ramparts of the Rubies, the Beaverhead country, the uplands of Horse Prairie, and Monida Pass in the Continental Divide. Ahead, somewhat north of the train, rose the mining country of Ruby River and its tributaries, the boom camps and towns, of which Virginia City, on the eastern slope of Mount Davidson, was the foremost.

Thirsty and bored, Ki sauntered up the aisle, eyeing the occupant of each seat as he moved to join the porter at the water cooler. The porter, smiling politely, shifted to the other side of the vestibule door, which was open on its catch-rod. Ki stepped to fill the paper pouch with water, and could now see that there were two men swaying on the open platform of the coach ahead.

One was a young redheaded lout, sunburned and peeling, an S&W Schofield .44, grips turned forward for a right-hand draw, under the waistband of his trousers on the left side. The second was thinner and perhaps a decade older, with a sallow, pitted face. A *very* sawed-off shotgun, of a style some fancied for brush work, was thonged with its double barrels downward under his thigh-length buffalo vest. Otherwise the two men were wearing nondescript range garb,

40

and Ki's initial impression was that they were ranch hands, outside taking the air.

Ki was just tilting his head to drink from the cup, when a third man came out on the next coach's platform. He had an instant's shadowed glimpse of a hatchet face, a beak of a nose, and a long-limbed body. It was the man he'd seen running from Thorian's house.

Recognition flashed in the man's narrowing eyes, and his mouth opened in a soundless snarl. He pivoted sideways, his long, dexterous fingers drawing a Colt revolver.

The porter was in the line of fire, but that wasn't stopping the man. "Down!" Ki cautioned, and swept the porter to the floor with his left forearm, as he sprang away from the water cooler, his right hand darting into his vest pocket for a *shuriken*.

Bullets shattered the cooler's glass bottle and gouged splinters from the woodwork above Ki when, crouching, he snapped off the *shuriken*. Somewhere in the coach a woman screamed, then he heard the *thwack!* as his spinning steel disk buried itself in solid bone. He hurled another, choking off the man's strangling cry, the man staggering against the railing, then flopping backward on the platform.

Even before the man had landed, a rapid hail of lead from the redhead's pistol was tunneling through the vestibule doorway. Ki flattened out, willing to wait for the erratic salvo to click empty, and wary of the second man's as-yet-unfired scattergun. A drummer close behind Ki was nailed and toppled with a low moan, just as the shooting ceased.

Then a coach door slammed. Ki peered up cautiously. He couldn't see anyone on the other platform now, but he was thinking he could hear running boots further ahead, when wails and shouts from his coach drowned them out. Four passengers, including Jessie, started toward him, and the porter scrambled for the emergency cord.

Ki yelled, "Stay there!" and sprinted out, vaulting from one platform railing across the couplers to the other, and dropping beside the dead body. It lay staring sightlessly, a *shuriken* sunk in the bridge of the nose, and another slicing tangentially through the base of the neck.

Ki paused, listening. But there was more noise than ever, the passengers from his own coach disregarding his order, and the passengers from this forward coach equally alarmed, both groups trying to crowd onto the platforms while talking all at once. From the engine a long whistle was sounding, and iron was squealing as brakes locked on.

The train shuddered in a spark-flaring slide, almost tripping Ki as he stepped toward the door. He wanted those two men. They'd sided the dead one, who he was convinced was the bomber; and they were loose on board, desperate and trigger-itchy. He wanted to find them, make them talk, stop them before they seized hostages or could jump from the gradually slowing train.

Then, abruptly, on Ki's left, a man bellowed out a window. A pistol cracked from trackside, and glass shattered. Ki dashed to the platform steps, grasping the handrail to brace himself against the coach's whiplashing pitch. Faintly he heard what sounded like scraping feet on the cinders. He clung for a moment, undecided, then swung from the handrail in a quick, twisting dive.

And gunfire erupted. Bullets plowed into wood paneling and rang against ironwork, pursuing Ki to the cinder bed with the hasty aim of a shootist caught unawares. Immediately Ki rolled under the coach, hearing behind him a peevish voice:

"Leave him be, Taylor, we gotta git!"

Ki squirmed fast across rails and ties, while carefully gauging the train's slackening speed. Crawling out on the other side, mere inches from the bladed flange of a wheel, he slewed up and into a crouching run toward the front of the now barely moving coach.

"Here, Max!" From around the back of the last coach, the redhead suddenly appeared at a lope. "The bastard's over here!"

Already the pistol was bucking in the redhead's fist, a swath of slugs drilling the cinders and ricocheting off the car trucks. Ki flung himself at a headlong angle beneath the coach again, cursing silently—that oaf was more persistent than accurate, but he was a fast shot, and had to be one of the fastest reloaders Ki had ever encountered.

Squirreling onto his back and catching hold of a crossmember, Ki lifted himself clear of the trackbed, letting the undercarriage carry him along. The redhead, kneeling, fired twice more at him. Metal sang with the slugs' impact—just as a pair of boots hurried past Ki. It had to be Max, the scattergun artist. Dropping, Ki quickly slid from the bed and out over the rail, then began snaking up behind him.

"Taylor, I'll go without you!" Max was threatening, angrily brandishing his scattergun at the passengers in the windows. "I will, dammit, I ain't stayin'—" As if he sensed someone coming at his back, he suddenly spun, whirling, leveling his scattergun.

Ki responded in a blur of motion. One driving step, two steps, and he clamped Max's triggering hand in a merciless vise of steely fingers. Max, reacting with swift savagery, looped a left-fisted roundhouse swing, while yanking his scattergun closer to knee Ki in the groin. But Ki turned a half-pace sideways, dodging the knee as he forearm-blocked the swing, then wrapped his free hand around Max's right elbow joint.

Guided by Ki, Max jerked up his scattergun and punched its twin muzzles brutally into his own throat—the most vulnerable spot, Ki believed, when it was necessary to temporarily silence and disable someone. Such as now. And the iron force of the barrels, crushing against his larynx, muted and stunned Max with paralyzing agony, and the scattergun slipped from his numb fingers, Ki taking possession of it with his left hand while shifting to chop Max unconscious with a *shuto* blow—

"He's mine! Get away!"

Ki swiveled around as Max had, fast, bringing the scattergun to bear. The redhead was trotting from behind the last coach again, nimbly inserting fresh rounds into his hinged-open pistol—a tempting target, but perhaps a bit too distant. Ki checked his impatience, leery of an unfamiliar weapon that was cut specially for spread instead of range.

"I've divvies on this scalp's bounty! Take caution, Max, I don't want to wing you!" That very instant the redhead snapped shut the cylinder, and Max be damned, the lead flew sizzling as he charged.

A bullet buzzed past his cheek, and Ki figured the redhead had come far enough. He triggered one barrel and felt the jarring recoil of black powder erupting fire and buckshot and gray smoke. A tortured shrieking arose, but Ki kept his finger on the scattergun's other trigger until the smoke dissipated sufficiently to see. The redhead was curled over, his arms hugging his belly as though he was sick to his stomach—which he was, there being a gaping crater and shredded meat where his abdomen should have been.

Immediately Ki triggered the other barrel to put the redhead out of his misery. There was no discharge. The hammer fell on an empty chamber or a defective shell.

He turned, then, back to Max. Max was gone. Hurriedly, Ki scanned the flanking underbrush, saw nothing, knew he'd heard nothing, and doubted that Max had had time to cross the trackbed's wide shoulder, particularly considering how dazed and weak and in pain from his injured throat he was. That left the train, which was finally easing to a full halt.

Hastening alongside, Ki surveyed the three coaches, their mostly closed windows crowded with faces. The

44

porters were evidently keeping tight rein on their alarmed and curious passengers, though; the vestibule doors were shut, and nobody was out riding on the platform decks.

"Stay inside!" Ki called up. "Stay inside, there's still one on the prowl or hiding here. Did anyone see which way he went?"

The faces nodded and shook their heads, declaring and gesturing in every conceivable direction. Just goes to prove, Ki thought sourly, the reliability of eye-witnesses. He'd deal with Max on his own.

He slowed, cradling the scattergun. It was useless to him, but he was unwilling to dump it someplace where Max might get it; Max might also have extra shells. Gliding as quietly as a shadow, his free hand always hovering by his vest, he began examining under and between the coaches, working toward the freight cars and engine, frequently glancing behind him.

The only person in sight was the redhead, now mercifully dead. His pistol was also in plain sight; Ki, having checked it early on, found it warped by buckshot, but left it as bait. He didn't think Max would be lured into the open by so bald a trick, yet he felt it was worth a try. He was more concerned that with the train stopped, Max could readily pass back and forth. He was near the baggage car, contemplating a climb to its roof deck for an overview, when he detected the sound of a coach vestibule door opening and closing.

Ki dipped down between the baggage car and the first boxcar.

Jessie peered out from the front platform of the last coach. After a pause, she stepped down and dropped to the cinders, then started rearward. Ki swung after her, but had taken perhaps six paces when he saw that she was being stalked. Max seemed to rise out of nowhere, though Ki suspected he'd glimpsed her from the other side and speedily crossed at the couplers.

"Jessie!" Ki tore into a run, tossing the scattergun aside, his own weapons impractical until he got closer. *"Jessie!"*

She heard Ki and wheeled. Max loomed over her, one hand clutching at her and the other rubbing his sore throat. Jessie backpedaled hastily and drew her .38 revolver. She fired, but Max spoiled her aim with a lunging, long-armed slap to her gunwrist, and her shot whistled by him. Before she could fire again, he seized her arm and twisted her around.

With Jessie now thrust between him and Max, Ki didn't dare risk using his weapons. And as long as she was locked in Max's arm-pinning hold, Jessie couldn't draw the derringer hidden behind her belt buckle. But making Jessie his shield was not Max's intention; he wanted her revolver. Frantically he groped and mauled her, wrenching her about as she resisted gamely, struggling in his frenzied grip.

Ki reached Max just as he was swinging Jessie from her feet. Ki's hand bit into the deep muscle crowning the ridge of Max's shoulder—a cruel, implacable bite of fingers, crippling in their savagery. Max freed Jessie, struggling to strike back at Ki. Ki turned him, spearing a stiff-fingered *yonhon-nukite* blow into his belly to bend him, and coldly chopped him into the cinders underfoot with the edge of a hand behind his ear.

Max huddled on one knee, head down, gasping. Ki nudged him with a toe, not gently. "Talk," he said tersely. "Who hired your friend, the bomber? Who set the scalp bounties? And why?"

Max grumbled an indistinct answer.

Ki glanced at Jessie; she countered with a light smile. She had stepped back against the coach and was watching silently, tapping the revolver softly yet irritably in her palm, but otherwise not betraying any agitation beyond the tense rise and fall of her breasts.

Ki nudged Max on the cinders again. "Talk."

Max gave a growly whimper this time. And because Max had been beaten twice within minutes and was abjectly crouching now, Ki was careless for an instant. As Ki's attention briefly flicked toward Jessie again, Max surged upright, flinging a handful of cinders in Ki's eyes. His hand kept on moving, sweeping out and snatching the revolver from Jessie's palm. Then he launched into a wild backward run to gain space, leveling the revolver.

By then, Ki was knuckling his eyes and cursing his folly. And Jessie was fit to swear too, but when Max began his fast backpedaling, she knew she'd never be able to draw her derringer in time, although she tried anyway. "Down! Down, quick!"

Ki would not go down. Instead he took Jessie high on the arm with his left hand and forced her downward, while with his right he whipped throwing daggers out from inside his vest, three of them, one at a time, still fighting the pain in his eyes.

His vision was blurred, but he threw well, because he could make out Max's form, and the gunman was no longer what Ki considered human. Twice he'd given Max the benefit of the doubt and spared his life, but matters were past that now, and Max was just a target.

Max fired, and if he felt anything about killing these two, it would have been joy. Ki's first throw and Max's gunshot occurred almost simultaneously, but Ki's blade was already buried in Max's heart when the gunman pulled the trigger, so the shot went wide, whining off into the clear air.

Max stepped back, dead, a half-pace, and Ki nailed him with the second and third knives as insurance.

Max came apart at the seams, collapsing across the roadbed shoulder, face up, one arm stretched out, with Jessie's revolver lying in his open palm like a gift.

"Thanks, Ki," Jessie said shakily. "Now I'll see if I can remove that grit from your eyes."

She probed delicately with a lace handkerchief at Ki's eyes and brought him instant relief. Ki went over to Max, retrieved his knives, and searched the killer's clothes. He didn't find anything, not so much as an extra shell for the scattergun, which at least explained why Max had been so stingy about firing the thing earlier.

Returning Jessie's revolver to her, Ki climbed up to the platform deck where the first man, the bomber, still sprawled. This body didn't yield any clues to its identity, either, but from the watch pocket of the bomber's denim trousers, Ki dug out a red pressboard token, like a poker chip, good for one free drink at the Silverado Club in Virginia City.

He was just completing his examination of the dead bomber when the vestibule door swung open, framing the pale faces of the conductor and the coach porter. The conductor was middle-aged and scrawny, but he puffed himself up like a bantam rooster in a henhouse.

"The Virginia & Truckee does not allow shooting on its rolling stock and properties," he said. "You're party to serious offenses."

"Not so fast," Ki said. "I don't carry a firearm."

The conductor scowled and brought a black notebook out of his uniform pocket. "Nevertheless, they were shooting at you. Why?"

Ki was forming a starchy response to that when Jessie stepped up onto the platform, pinned the conductor with a frigid eye, and said, "It is blatantly obvious to anyone with a brain that this gentleman foiled a train robbery. And singlehandedly, I might add. The Virginia & Truckee did nothing to intercede, and in fact the only action the Virginia & Truckee seems to have taken is to permit the bandits on. And punch their tickets. Is this the way your clumsy railroad always operates?"

"We, ah . . . we have strict regulations, ma'am. Strict regulations and requirements, I assure you." The conductor scribbled distractedly in his book, and behind him the porter secretly grinned. "I'm afraid we will have to notify the proper authorities in Virginia City," he continued apologetically. "Just a formality, I assure you, but where a killing is involved—"

"Yes, yes," Jessie cut in wearily. "If we should ever arrive there. We must be stopping at every gopher hole along the line."

The conductor beat a hasty retreat after that, but having been left with no place to vent his own irritation, he chewed into the porter as they left. "Intolerable, Ralph, this laxness must cease. We must maintain prompt schedules and regular stops, you hear? Now, you and Sam, and Wiley too, fetch those bodies to the baggage car, pronto..."

Smiling blithely, Jessie stepped down from the platform to cross over to the rear car again. Ki followed a moment later, after he contemplated the red saloon token he had taken from the dead bomber's pocket. It made him wonder about Francine Mac-Near...

★

Chapter 5

Shortly after the train was under way, it made another
brief unscheduled stop, this time at a lonely telegraph
relay station. When Jessie asked, the porter explained
that the conductor was having a message dispatched
to the Storey County authorities.

The train climbed sharply after that, the labored
puffing of the locomotive roiling back in noisy gusts
as they slid around curves. The green mountainous
terrain all around was increasingly slashed with manmade scars. Virginia City's environs were more of
the same, they saw—a concentration of callously
gouged slashes and waste dumps of tailings, bleak
monuments to man's greed for the wealth of the earth's
buried ore.

The tracks to the depot ran along the middle of a
busy street. The street, in turn, ran through the middle
of Virginia City, dividing an upper district of respectable homes from a dingy slum area below. On both
sides the sloping land was hatched with terraced lanes

50

and steep stairways, and pocked with mineshafts and tunnels, making Virginia City resemble a human prairie-dog town.

With bell tolling and steamcocks hissing, the train shivered to a halt. A coroner's muledrawn hearse was waiting to remove the corpses from the baggage car, and a taciturn deputy took charge of Ki as soon as he alighted. Accompanied by Jessie, the deputy escorted Ki across the depot to a white-haired oldster with the bowed legs of a wrangler and the massive shoulders of a miner. A marshal's badge was pinned to the vest of his somber blue-black town suit.

The marshal nodded but otherwise ignored them, his attention monopolized by the man facing him, a stocky, unkempt, grizzled fellow with a mouth that was fat-lipped and roaring.

"Ain't one to pick on cripples," the man was bellowing when they approached, "but lately he's been wideloopin' me blind, Tilden!"

"Any proof against Mastleg, Noah?"

"Well, me an' my crew ain't seen him do it, or found no carcasses, either. But the only way sheep can get lifted outta my valley is north. Ain't a cut east or south to herd 'em through the hills, and from my ranch at the west mouth, we can spot anything comin' or going. That leaves north, where there's a path goin' over a low saddleback and across his claim. Hell, it's just common sense that he's the one rustlin' my stock, or is in cahoots with whoever is."

"Seems sensible," the marshal allowed. "But common sense don't stand up in court, Noah. You gotta show solid facts for proof."

"It won't *need* to stand up in court, when I'm done gettin' proof! When I catch that lobo, I'll strip his hide for a fact! I'll—"

"Noah Winthrop, you take the law into your own hands, and by gum, you'll end up in court yourself." The marshal scowled and tugged on his lapel. "Now,

51

in a day or so, I'll go have a palaver with Mastleg, and comb around his digs for sign of your mutton, okay?"

"Fat chance of a find," Winthrop retorted caustically. "He's been butcherin' 'em and hawkin' 'em to the miners as fast as he swipes 'em, I damn well know he has. And you'd best stop him fast, Tilden, else I'll do some butcherin' myself!" With that, Winthrop heeled about and stalked away.

Watching the sheep rancher go, Marshal Tilden said to his deputy, "Those two have been feuding for years, mostly for their own amusement, though they're too stubborn to admit it. But if Mastleg is stealing more'n an occasional meal, their fussing could turn serious."

"Yes sir. I brung you that Mr. Ki from the train, sir."

Turning, Tilden regarded Ki, then Jessie. "Before I hear witnesses," he said, his honest steel-blue eyes raking Ki again without fear or favor, "I want to hear your version."

Ki told him what had happened, carefully omitting any mention of the bombing in Reno.

"It's a bad business," Tilden said then. "Very awkward."

That was not what Jessie and Ki wanted to hear. Cases weightier than the local garden variety could slow a frontier legal machine to a glacial pace. Jessica, foreseeing endless dispositions and interrogations, countered, "It's self-defense, and very simple!"

"I'm sure, ma'am. But I ain't the coroner, and his inquest will take more convincing. Your friend'll have to stay a few days, so no offense, but I'd like to know what y'all had in mind to do."

Jessie handed him the photo. "We're looking for Unity Balsam."

"Enoch Balsam's child?" He eyed the photo as if it were a curio, then returned it and, shaking his head, took out an old briar pipe and a tobacco pouch. "Can't say I wish you luck, or to hear another word about it. That gored a bunch of us, that mess back then, and left some raw wounds yet. Forget what you want, and let the dead get to dying." He thumbed black plug into the bowl, staring at something they couldn't see. "It's rotten here. Too much money afloat, and too many folks preferring to steal it than earn it. I'm getting tired, mighty tired." He paused until his pipe was going, then used it to gesture pointedly at Ki. "I won't jug you, you're free on your honor as long as you stay out of trouble. Take my advice and check into the Palace, order drinks sent to your room, and stay there ordering drinks."

Ki grinned. "Well, it's a bit early for a bender."

Tilden blew some smoke. "Not in Virginia City, it isn't."

They parted, the marshal going with his deputy to interview the conductor, while Jessie and Ki took him up on his advice, arranging to have their luggage delivered to the Palace Hotel.

The Palace was good advice. Standing prominently on Idaho Street, it boasted a ballroom lobby with potted palms and a snotty clerk in a morning coat. The bar was on one side, the restaurant on the other, and there were plenty of plush-carpeted rooms for distinguished guests in the spacious wings and floors above.

Once they'd checked into their adjoining east-wing rooms, Jessie and Ki disregarded the rest of Tilden's advice. They went out, following the clerk's directions to the ramshackle publishing shop of the *Territorial Enterprise*. A five-dollar tip later, they were in a musty room, sifting through back issues. Eventually they located a series of articles dating from the train heist on through to the escape, but the stories were generally repetitious, smothering bits of fresh news in reams of rewritten copy. When they finally left, they were wiser for knowing the siege had lasted all of four days and nights, with the robbers holed up

53

in a rugged section claimed by Enoch Balsam—referred to by the *Enterprise* as "that debt-nagged, land-poor brigand of the barren Monteplata Mines."

The blue dusk was beginning to sift down from the hills as they walked back to the hotel, measuring the town and its inhabitants. Pedestrians hurried, even when they apparently had no particular place to go. There were barkers standing on soap boxes, shouting claims of available work in the mines and ore mills, or the wood ranches near Lake Tahoe. The roadways teemed with saddle horses, buggies, and enormous freight wagons. The loud, imaginative profanity of teamsters added color to the general hubbub.

Large false-fronted emporia shone with paint and plate glass, and ornate bars and gaming halls catered to the snobs of the Exchange and Millionaire Row. The garish saloons and honkytonks of the lower elevations were packed and roaring, especially the impressive Silverado Club, whose entrance was flanked by flaming torches and guarded by a malevolent-looking pirate wearing an eyepatch and two pistols.

The Palace's elegant dining room was a marvel of white linen, sparkling silver, black-coated waiters, and a gourmet menu. The faint strains of a cello and flute could be heard in the background, while, a few short blocks away, men were being mugged for beer money.

Virginia City was velvet and sewage, jewels and belly guns, handshakes and cold steel in the back. As in Reno, Jessie and Ki kept a sharp lookout for any killer on the prowl. But in Virginia City they were finding that they could take their pick of several dozen, with the number mounting steadily.

After they finished their dessert and coffee, Ki rose and motioned to Jessie to stay seated. "Here's where we separate the men from the ladies," he said wryly. "Relax while I go scout out the Silverado. Oh—let me borrow the photo, will you?"

She handed it to him. "For what, I can't imagine."

"I can't either, but it can't hurt to have it just in case."

"Well, don't lose it." She smiled teasingly. "And don't come in late. Within an hour, I think, before you can cause trouble and land in jail. One hour, and then I'll come get you. Just in case."

"If I'm not back in an hour, Jessie, bring the cavalry."

The lights of Virginia City were stars in a deep purplish haze now, and a cool breeze wafted through the hodgepodge of streets. A fistfight was in full swing next to a gin dive, and the tinny blare of off-key music from dance halls vibrated the air, almost deafening Ki to any sounds of stealthy approach.

The interior of the Silverado was much as he'd expected. The walls of the large frame building were lined with plush fabric, wagon-wheel chandeliers hung low and smoky from a latticework ceiling, and the crowded mahogany bar was being serviced by three nubile brunettes in cancan skirts. The opposing wall of poker tables, chuckaluck setups, and wheels of fortune was equally crowded. Some dozen girls were working that stretch and the main floor, cadging as many drinks as they served, also dressed in cancan skirts, net stockings, and buckle shoes. They wore nothing above the waist, and seemed to be enjoying their semi-nudity and the bug-eyed reactions they got from the throngs of miners, laborers, and unattached townsmen. For married men, the Silverado was off limits.

Ki chose a side table and ordered bottle beer from a chubby-breasted, henna-haired waitress. He paid cash, saving the red token. It probably meant nothing. Free-drink chips were common, and probably the bomber had passed through here once. And probably Ki's meeting Francine while she was traveling here was coincidental, too. Sure.

Returning, the waitress sat down. "A gal do get a thirst."

Ki grinned genially. "I'm broke."

She was up and gone before the foam could settle in his glass. Ki eased back, nursed his beer, and gazed around. On a small stage across the room, three pretty girls playing bass, banjo, and fiddle were whomping out a square-dance medley. They were dressed in fringed buckskin skirts and cowboy boots and, like the bartenders and waitresses, were naked from the navel up. They weren't bad musicians, either.

Ki sat, content to wait. Sooner or later he'd learn if and how this deadfall might be significant. He must have waited twenty minutes before the door at the end of the bar opened and a man came out.

The man was short and pudgy, in gray suit trousers and shirtsleeves. He looked fortyish, a clipped mustache accentuating the roundness of his face, his dark hair pomaded across a thinning spot, his black eyes ebullient as he toured the backbar, then began strolling through the main area.

A high-tone pimp, Ki thought; a pimp and a shark of an owner. A popular one too, chucking this girl under the chin, patting that girl on the fanny.

Making his rounds, the man had approached to within six feet of Ki, when he was joined by another man. The second was knobby-thin and had the pointy face of a possum; his brown hair was long, his cheap range garb was dirty, and there was nothing prepossessing about him. Except that his revolver, a Remington Improved Army .45, was stuck higher, odder, than the normal casual way of sticking it in one's trousers. It had probably fooled a few men into overconfidence, but it warned Ki that the man had a holster inside his pants, rigged for a quick draw.

The second man smiled. "A man livin' by odds should keep his mind on the game, Grantree. There could be some rule changes comin'."

The first man, Grantree, became very still. He said something low to the second man that Ki couldn't

56

catch, and walked toward his office. The second man hesitated, then followed him.

When the office door closed on the pair, Ki returned to eyeing the trio with benevolent interest. They were playing cowboy ballads now, with the emphasis on the wailing fiddle. Indeed, the fiddler appeared to be the leader of the trio, likely because she was the tallest, perhaps five-eight or five-ten, generously breasted, with her other curves nicely proportioned for her size. Her wheat-blond hair was coiled around her head in sleek yellow ropes and secured by tiny combs; it framed pleasantly stimulating features, especially her saucerlike eyes.

They ended the song and relaxed. Ki continued dwelling on the fiddler, and suddenly a ridiculous notion flashed through his mind. But by then the trio had left the stage to take a break, filing out through a burgundy velvet drape, presumably to dressing rooms in back.

Ki sat impatiently, listening to the barroom noises and wanting the trio's loud rhythms, eager for the intermission to end. He almost missed seeing Francine as she scampered up to his table.

He grinned. "You said if I ever got to Virginia City—"

"But what a shock! I come on duty, and here you are." She smiled, waggling her serving tray. "C'mon, buy me my first drink."

Ki agreed to buy one of the outrageously expensive champagne cocktails. When Francine came back and sat down, she said, "Hard to believe, you being here sooner'n me. And easier, I bet. I swan, the men a girl has to put ou—" She stopped, sipped hastily. "God, that's vile, too. Well, now, why are you in town? Business?"

"Why, yes—to see the blond fiddler. Do me a favor, Francine, and go ask her if I can visit for a few minutes, will you?"

"Well, I like that fine howdy-do!"

"Strictly business." Ki leaned closer. "What's her name?"

"I don't know. I haven't been here long myself, you know. But I've already been warned not to allow callers backstage."

"She'll see me." Ki laid two twenty-dollar gold pieces and the torn picture on the table. "Here, just to try. And show her the picture and ask, that's all. You show her, and she'll see me."

"Well—" Francine eyed the photo dubiously, then conceded, scooping up the coins. "I'll try, Ki. One try, no guarantees."

Ki watched her wind between the crowded tables to one side of the stage, where she slipped through the burgundy velvet drape. He surveyed the barroom until she reappeared, which wasn't long. She threaded her way back, smiling, and said, "Number eight, killer."

He retrieved the photo and thanked her, then walked across to the side of the stage. Behind the drape was a drab corridor lined with doors. Some doors were open, and from some of those came girlish voices. Door number eight was closed, but it was thin, and Ki caught muffled splashing sounds and a woman's voice singing a ballad.

He knocked. The singing became a call: "Enter!"

The interior of the room was small, with two glowing hobnail lamps, a mirrored vanity, a wardrobe, and a bunk-sized bed. At the far end was a three-wing screen, from behind which was coming the splashing.

She asked, "Are you Ki? The one who sent the picture?"

"Yes. Sorry to intrude. I'm looking for Unity Balsam."

"All right, I'll be right out."

He could hardly believe he'd found her so easily, though his Japanese heritage taught him that there was really no such thing as a coincidence, and that when a man was ready to find what he was searching for, it would come to him almost effortlessly. Of course, his sharp Westerner's eye for detail hadn't hurt, either. When he'd seen her eyes, he'd known immediately that they were the same eyes as those of the little girl in the photo, though older and definitely sadder. And she did resemble her mother, whom he'd glimpsed so briefly in reversed image at Thorian's house in Reno. He realized that Marshal Tilden must have known she was here, yet had lied to spare her further pain. The only really startling thing was the fact that Francine had told him of this place, and then he'd found that token in the dead bomber's pocket. Well, the world was full of surprises...

"I get so hot and stinky out there," Unity said as she walked out from behind the partition. "So I take sponge baths during my breaks."

She was dripping wet and wearing nothing except a towel. It wasn't a big towel, and she didn't try to hide behind it as she began to dry her legs. Up close, without a screen of tobacco and lamp smoke, Ki could see the detailed curves of her high full breasts, slim waist, and smooth opulent hips. Yet, as before, her impact lay in her eyes, those deep, melancholy pools of azure blue, which Ki found very feminine. Very exciting.

She smiled apologetically, misreading Ki's expression. "You're embarrassed. I'm sorry. You see, I'm virtually like this every evening, so I'm apt to forget."

"I'm admiring, not upset. You're lovely to look at."

"It's not too bad, is it?" she said gravely, gazing down at her body. "Better than when I was ten. Where'd you get my picture?"

"From a dead crook."

She regarded Ki, mockery mixed with her gravity now. "I see you have a poor sense of humor, Mr. Ki."

"Ki, no 'mister,'" he replied, shaking his head.

"I'm not kidding, Unity. The dead man I'm talking about is one of seven deaths connected somehow with the photo. That is, seven which we—my friend, Miss Jessica Starbuck, and myself—which we know about. We want to discover the connection and stop the deaths. That's why I'm here, Unity. We want to learn how and from whom the dead man got your picture."

For a moment she stared at Ki, sober and intent. "You aren't lying to me. But I don't know. The picture is one my mother had. I'm afraid if you want to speak to her, it'll be over her grave."

"I'm sorry."

"Don't be. She wasn't. She was loyal and faithful to my father, and when he was—when he died, she took over working his claims. The claims are worthless. She didn't fold." Unity stood there, now briskly toweling her breasts. "She remarried two years ago, to Mr. Thistle, who's not old, really. But he's lived hard and suffers from a bad leg, so before long, Mama wound up working the claims again. When she could stand it no longer, she lay down, slept, and died."

"Do you have her effects?"

"No. What there was—damn little—is with Thistle at the cabin." She went behind the screen and began putting on her skirt. "I'll take you out there tomorrow, if you like. Both of you, in the morning. Say, about nine?"

"Thanks. Isn't it a little early for you?"

"It's so sweet of you to be concerned," she replied wryly, moving over to sit down at her vanity. "But my little group is only one of the attractions, and not a main one at that. I work afternoons through evenings, and get off at ten, so I'll get my sleep."

"Tell me, do you like this sort of life?" Ki asked.

"You're smarter than that."

"Maybe," Ki answered, "but are you? Don't you get lonely?"

Unity gave him a sardonic glance. "Mister, who would marry a girl from the Silverado Club?" She

60

rose abruptly and adjusted her skirt. "I've got to get the group going, before we get fired."

Ki escorted her back along the corridor after she closed and padlocked her door. Unity, Ki saw as they walked together, had a grace of carriage and an innate freshness not commonly found in women working in deadfalls like this.

"I work here because I can't work mining," Unity was telling him. "I wouldn't if I could. I don't want to kill myself like Mama. Grantree offered me a job that pays better than most, and doesn't get ideas. It's like marrying, Ki. Who'd hire the daughter of a lynched robber?"

He nodded. So she had made her way on her own, as best she could. He held the drape aside for her. "If you're free after you get off at ten..."

She hesitated on the stage side of the drape, humor warming the blue of her eyes. "No, at nine. Tomorrow morning, at Flynn's Livery."

Ki chuckled. "We'll be there."

Her two partners were already onstage, waiting. Unity moved around to the steps at stage center, then paused to call out to Ki, "Just 'cause I play the fiddle, Ki, doesn't mean I fiddle around."

"I'll remember that." It was probably the soundest piece of advice he'd receive about this girl, he decided, watching Unity mount the stage and pick up her instrument.

Chapter 6

Jessie, aghast at the price, looked from the two rental bay mares and snapped, "I see not all the thieves here wear guns!"

The toothless old hostler cackled at her outraged expression. "Feed comes high. Everything hasta be freighted in. You want 'em?"

A voice said, "Won't do you any good to try elsewhere."

Turning, Jessie and Ki saw Unity walking a splotched pinto out of the livery stable. "The others charge more and don't take as good care," she continued, jiggering her horse across the wide front yard to them. "That's why I suggested Flynn's to Ki last night."

"Good morning," Ki greeted her. "Did you beat us here by long?"

"Morning. No, I was saddling my horse in back when you arrived."

Jessie was paying as Flynn said cheerfully, "It's less if you keep 'em by the week."

"These nags should live so long," Jessie replied as she and Ki mounted the creaky saddles and, alongside Unity, trotted out into the flow of jostling traffic.

Ki formally introduced the two women as Unity directed them southwestward. The sun was rising over the Tobacco Root Mountains in the east, and was beginning to highlight the Rubies and distant Rockies, while they left Virginia City behind them on a rough, potholed wagon road. Flanking them were numerous tents and shacks, the hillsides gouged and pitted, the streams laced and cluttered with sluices and pans, screens and Long Toms and gravel piles. The era of fabulous strikes and overnight wealth was past, but a prospector could still pan or dig himself a large day's pay here if he was willing to work.

After a while the sprawl of claim sites grew thinner as the road increasingly split into trails to remote camps and settlements. Conversation had lagged by now. Unity was friendly but not very chatty, and though Jessie had been trying to draw her out, she hadn't been forthcoming with much more than she'd already told Ki.

In fact, Unity's casual reserve would never have revealed that she might be the key to murder. Her only oddity, Jessie thought, was how she had combined a town-style red cape with a man's checked shirt, corduroy pants, and ankle-high Congress boots. A well-used Winchester .44-40 carbine rode in a saddle boot near her right thigh.

The road wound deeper into the foothills, through a sort of no-man's-land that lay relatively close to plenty of claims, yet free of any of them. Suddenly Jessie's mare grew skittish, and Jessie, reining in tight, said, "Pull up—quick!"

Halting with Unity, Ki asked, "What's wrong, Jessie?"

"My horse smells something up ahead, around that bend."

Unity shrugged. "Probably just some riders coming."

"Probably," Ki agreed, though he was thinking it could just as easily be another trap as he heeled his horse forward. "We'll see."

No riders appeared rounding the curve. Nobody seemed to be lurking in the surrounding brush and timber, either. Jessie, following Ki with Unity right behind, was starting to believe her bay had overreacted to some animal in the growth, when they reached the bend and glimpsed four men a short distance ahead.

The four were in a small clearing, grouped about a large oak that grew at the point where the trail forked. They were all on horseback, three of them with flour sacks over their heads, facing the fourth. He had his head twisted by the pressure of a noose around his neck, his hands tied behind him, and a cardboard square with some words printed on it pinned to the breast of his tan flannel shirt.

Unity gasped, shocked. "Gabe!"

She started to spur her horse ahead, but Jessie grasped the pinto's headstall and stopped her. "If we rush them, he'll get shot, or his horse will spook and hang him anyway."

"But we've got to—" Unity began, then saw that Ki was already acting, albeit slowly, nonchalantly moseying toward the group.

Ki would have moved faster if this had been the usual quick lynching. But there was some delay, as one of the hooded men did a lot of talking to the prisoner. Ki was too far away to hear the words, but he could see the prisoner shaking his blanched face.

"Hello the hanging!" Ki called out heartily, as if he were nearing a stranger's cabin. "Is this the path to Finagle's camp?"

The hooded men cursed, and there was a sudden

jostling of their horses, of hands fumbling toward sidearms. One was a hulking giant, another of medium size and shape, the third rather thin and lanky, straddling a line-backed grulla. It was the third who responded to Ki with a single barked command: "Git the hell gone!"

Ki slowed to a halt, close now, and slightly to one side of the tree. He looked as if his feelings had been hurt. Jessie's mare, under the concealed jab of her heel, shied worse than before; her face took on a half-frightened expression when her mount started prancing, but changed to relief when she'd calmed it to a stop just on the other side of the tree from Ki.

Ki said amiably, "There's nothing I like better than unmannerly, rude people. I feel I've done a service when I beat them till the devil won't have it."

"Why, you slant-eyed shit, I'll—" the lanky man began. But he didn't finish. With the three men's attention diverted by Ki, Jessie had no problem drawing her revolver and thumbing back its hammer.

"Yes?" she said, training the revolver on them.

Unity came in during the momentary silence. Almost casually, but with a smoothness that was swifter than it looked, she slid out her carbine and centered it on the lanky man. Her voice was a purr:

"Party's over, gents. Move off, and keep moving. I can hit a running coyote four out of five times at a hundred yards with this."

The lanky man's eyes flashed behind the cut-out eyes of his hood, and black rage made him stiff in the saddle. Ki's gaze had not wavered from him, sensing something familiar about the man, yet the single peculiarity he noticed was that the man wasn't wearing a pistol.

Throaty with anger, the man snarled, "You got us whipsawed this time. But I promise you, it ain't the end. No man—or woman—can meddle in the affairs of the Posse. You'll be dealt with later!"

He lifted his arm and the three swung their horses. They headed down one of the forks, toward a nearby line of ridges.

Ki coaxed his horse closer and unsheathed the short, curved *tanto* knife he wore behind his belt. Reaching out, he slashed the taut rope, the noose falling slack. The prisoner swayed in his saddle.

"I owe you one," he panted gratefully. He was in his mid-twenties, Ki judged, a handsome strapper with a cleft chin, a straight thin nose, and eyes that were dark and hard. "Pounced on me outta the rocks, strung me up, and I reckoned I was a goner."

By then Unity was pressing alongside, untying his hands. "You fool," she kept muttering, her voice trembling. "Gabe, you damn fool."

"Aw, Unity, don't claw. How was I to know?"

Ki removed the noose with its big, clumsy hangman's knot, and took out the horseshoe nail pinning the cardboard square. On it were a crudely drawn skull and crossbones and the numerals "3 – 7 – 77"—the dimensions of a grave, three feet wide, seven feet long, and seventy-seven inches deep. He passed the square to Jessie, then turned to the man again, who was patting Unity's hand reassuringly.

"My name's Gabe Winthrop," the man said when Unity pushed his hand aside. He nodded, grinning, as Jessie and Ki introduced themselves. "I'd better join you, if you don't mind. You headin' to Unity's claim?"

"To Thistle's, not mine," Unity rebuked, and started along the other fork. Gabe fell in with Jessie and Ki, sighing the way men do when they don't understand women. "You'd think it was my fault, eh?"

Jessie asked, "What were they hanging you for?"

"Claim-jumpin'. Which is plumb nervy of them, it being my claim. Well, actually I leased it from Unity's stepdad. They was tryin' to jump it themselves, to make me sign the lease over. Me, I figured as soon as I did, I'd get stretched, so I was refusin'."

"Smart thinking," Ki said. "The one who was doing the talking spoke of a posse, and that was a vigilante-style warning they'd pinned on you. Is that what they're passing themselves off as — vigilantes?"

"Yeah, Posse Comitatus they calls it. It's only a cover for finding ways to fill their own pockets, though, a blind for killing and robbing any prospectors they reckon have a stake worth grabbing."

Ahead, Unity twisted around. "You mean your claim is paying?"

"Nope, not yet!" Gabe answered cheerily. "'Course, I just started working it, but they musta heard I was onto a sure strike."

"Damn all," Unity said. "They've been riding roughshod for five or six months now, and it's high time the Posse was smashed. And I'd like to do the smashing."

"First, Unity, you gotta know who and where they are."

Conversation lagged, the trail narrowing to single-file passage. They descended a slope for several miles and entered a gloomy gorge, which in time widened into an easy-graded pass along the north side of a low range of hills. A couple of miles farther on, the trail angled through the hills, crested a rise, and dropped steeply into a rocky hollow. Midway across the hollow, a shallow ford spanned a swift white-water stream.

"Dishwater Creek," Unity explained as they crossed, and swung her arm, pointing eastward. "That high peak on our right is where Papa bought all his land, figuring to hit a lode like the Comstock. On this side is the main Monteplata claim, where my stepfather lives."

Gabe added, "I got my digs over 'cross on the southwestern flank. On t'other side, way east, some dude leased a whole big patch of claims."

Jessie, wanting to confirm what she already suspected, asked Gabe, "What lies south of the Monteplata land, just below you?"

"Well, my pa's herding sheep there. He's leased an upcountry valley there, so the graze is pretty thatchy, but the Dishwater runs through it, so water's a-plenty." Gabe Winthrop barked a laugh. "And beyond that is nothin'. The railroad curves in over there somewhere, but his only road loops a far piece afore it gets down into Dayton."

Again the four lapsed into silence, riding on toward the peak through a series of rounded canyons and rolling ridges. Occasionally the hillsides were blotched with overgrown tunnel and shaft openings, indicating, Jessie surmised, where Enoch Balsam had prospected and given up. His Monteplata landscape was left in desolate brooding, scarred by the passage of the man's failed dream.

They were descending yet another slope, the trail seeming to weave aimlessly, when they heard the rattle of gunfire close ahead. Without a word, Unity kicked her pinto into a gallop. Gabe, Jessie, and Ki launched themselves after her, following her flying red cape down through the concealing screen of trees and underbrush. Voices could be heard, bellowing in anger, but mostly the crash of guns echoed up at them.

Reaching bottom, they sped along the base of a ravaged, black-pitted cliff. At the far end, past slag heaps littered with refuse, stood a squat log cabin in a stump- and boulder-strewn clearing, with a stream trickling nearby, bordered by willow and witch hobble.

The volley of shots had died, and in the hush that followed, Jessie and Ki recognized Noah Winthrop's foghorn yell: "This mornin's been just a sample, Mastleg! We can keep you penned in till hell freezes over! You're bogged down, and you orter 'fess up to it!"

"The hell I will!" a gravelly voice shouted. There was the squeak of door hinges and an odd clumping noise, then, "Go on and do your li'l do, swabby! I'm

nestin' plump, with plenty fodder for my ol' Peabody!"

Closing, they now could see Winthrop and two
others, dismounted and fanned out behind the rocks,
eyes and weapons trained on the cabin.

Standing defiantly in the doorway was a bald, clean-
shaven man, short and plumpish, with the hardness
of a billiard ball. He wore a knotted bandanna around
his forehead, a grubby striped blazer, and wide, floppy-
bottomed, once-white sailor britches, the right leg of
which was cut off at the knee—if he'd had a knee.
From there down he possessed a peg leg, ornately
lathed like the leg of a fancy table.

He also possessed, clutched at the ready, a vintage
single-shot Peabody rifle. Uneasiness seemed to ripple
through the besiegers now, at mention of the .45/70/
480 rimfire cartridges used to stoke it.

"You won't torch that cannon at us," Winthrop
blustered with a touch of scorn. "It's agin your religion
to kill people, Mastleg!"

"The Good Book says, 'I give ye power to tread
on serpents and scorpions,'" Mastleg retorted, his
raspy voice rising, as Unity and then Gabe plowed to
a halt and hit the ground running. "So c'mon, you
clan o' pizenous sidewinders, and feel me do some
dead-center treadin'!"

Winthrop cursed, whiskers bristling. "Drive him
in and flat, boys! Cut that damn shack of his in two
and bring it down 'round his fat head!"

Gun-thunder rolled again, as repeaters and revolvers blistered the cabin's log walls and hastily slammed
door. The remaining pane of a window dissolved; the
stovepipe toppled in a cloud of soot. Then the barrel
of the Peabody poked out the broken window, erupted
with a roar, and one of Winthrop's boys let out a bleat
as over an ounce of lead plucked his hat away.

Above the furor, Unity and Gabe couldn't be heard.
Yet, plunging forward, risking injury if not outright

69

death, they thrust into the thick of the fray where they couldn't help but be seen. Jessie and Ki had dismounted by now and were a couple of paces behind, utterly ignored as the shooting abruptly ceased, the rifle vanishing from the window, and Winthrop and his boys rearing, staring in astonishment.

"Why, it's our young'un and the gal!" the hatless one blurted. And it was then, suddenly, that Jessie realized the two men with Winthrop were older brothers of Gabe. "What in tunket you doin' here?"

"And well I should ask you that!" Gabe snapped, and was about to add more, when the door opened and Mastleg clomped outside—the sight of whom caused Unity to order crisply, "Put your gun away, Thistle!"

"Not hardly, m'lass, not while confrontin' pirates!"

"Pirates! You thievin' horn toad!" Winthrop bawled. "Quit stealin' from my flocks, or I'll slice you off at your other knee!"

Mastleg Thistle spat noisily. "C'mencin' when?"

"Stop it!" Gabe demanded. "Shake yourselves together."

"I druther shake Mastleg apart," the brother with a hat growled. "He slipped up on me and Purdy last night, when we was tendin' sheep. We chanced to meet by a tree that was next to some brush, and it was sorta dark there. I didn't know nothin' till Purdy grunted, and when I looked to see what was wrong, I got whonked on the head. When we come to, we find we'd been sheared of a prime ewe and two lambs."

"You didn't see him? How d'you know it was Mastleg?" Gabe asked.

"Listen to my turncoat whelp of a son!" Winthrop exploded. "'Tain't enough he goes broke minin' instead of stickin' to a respectable family trade! 'Tain't enough he goes courtin' my worstest enemy's child! Oh no, now he's sassin' back, disbelievin' his own kin!"

"I'm only askin' you, all of you, to be sensible,"

70

Gabe replied evenly. "S'pose you an' Mastleg cool off awhile and give it a thinkin'."

"I don't hafta do no thinkin' t' know that I ain't lettin' him—"

"Waitin' a few days won't hurt nothin'," Gabe pressed on. "It maybe won't change nothin', either, but you won't be changin' nothin' here an' now, Paw, what with Miss Unity and me in your way."

Winthrop struggled to contain his fury, but finally acceded. "Okay, we'll be gettin' home. This just delays the fact," he warned, as the three gathered reins and mounted their horses. He glowered at Mastleg. "The fact that when I get my mitts on you, you low-livered, sneaky warthog, I'll skin you up till you look like a barber pole!"

The Winthrops headed out in a fast, dust-pluming gallop.

A splutter of cussing followed them, Mastleg Thistle spewing a strange combination of seafaring and Biblical profanities until they were gone from view. Then the change in Mastleg was immediate and startling. He propped his rifle inside the doorway, and his features relaxed into a broad grin as he gestured for them to enter.

"Well, come aboard, mateys, come aboard!"

Chapter 7

They filed through the doorway, Unity introducing
Jessie and Ki to her stepfather, then asking him, "Are
Mama's things still here?"

"Aye, where she left 'em, under m' bed," Mastleg
answered, sitting down and motioning for the others
to take chairs from the table.

Unity went to the rumpled, unmade bed, stooped
over, and dragged out a small crystallized metal trunk.
From what Jessie could glimpse, the trunk had been
neatly packed. The rest of the cabin was more in
accord with the bed; the home that Adabelle Balsam
had once kept so clean was now as filthy as a pigsty.
Empty bottles and tins and cast-off socks and old
longjohns cluttered the floor. Handmade rag rugs and
lace curtains were ruined. Tobacco and whiskey stains
were everywhere. The only saving grace was the large
cast-iron pot slowly simmering on the three-hole cookstove; the odor of whatever was cooking inside it was
succulent and mouth-watering.

Gabe was eyeing Mastleg coldly. "Stealing sheep again, eh?"

Mastleg, taking out a packet of brown cornhusk papers, glanced at Jessie. "My, if you ain't got a hull worthy of a clipper."

"Thistle!" Unity rebuked him while searching the trunk.

"Pshaw, m' lass, an old salt spies a trim ship, and he admires her. Same with a lady, that's all." He scrutinized Ki next, sighing. "To look at you makes me remember twenty years ago, when I was on shore leave in Hong Kong and Singapore and other ports where East meets West."

Gabe stood up. "Answer my question, Mastleg."

"Well, on occasion a sheep has strayed within range of my carving knife," he admitted, spilling tobacco in one paper. "But your dad's actual losses, Gabe, don't amount to a hill o' tailings."

"His profits don't, either. Those sheep are his margin."

"He's makin' it pay, and face it, at times his methods ain't any more honest than mine. Only the tough survive, to use Enoch's motto."

Unity slammed the trunk shut. "Keep my father out of it," she snapped, crossing to give Ki a photograph. "Is this what you wanted?"

Puzzled, Ki regarded a full, unripped print of the old family portrait. "Not exactly. What we want is a line on the torn picture," he said, handing the photo to Jessie, who added, "Thorian mentioned he made two copies back then, so who else would have been given one?"

"Papa, I imagine, to carry with him. Yes, I seem to recall—" She paused, shaking her head. "I know I never saw it after he, ah—afterwards." She hesitated again, then brightened. "It's noon, and we all must be starved. Thistle, what's cooking in the pot?"

Very low, he muttered: "Lamb stew."

"Figures. I'll ladle us some, soon's I wash up."

While Unity was outside, scrubbing bowls and utensils in the stream, Mastleg confided, "A nasty time, his death, accordin' to her ma. The railroad and mines sued to take the Monteplata as part restitution for what was robbed. They didn't get it, Enoch having died before bein' judged guilty of any crime. Adabelle still had to hire a lawyer, though, and had to give over a bunch of stuff to pay him."

"Including Balsam's personal effects?" Ki asked.

"Well, the lawyer, Lou Heiligman, was Enoch's size in clothes. Lou died last Christmas Eve; broke his neck when he fell drunk into a mine pit. A new fellow, Chester Neville, promptly hung out his shingle in Lou's place. Real sharp. Talked Gabe into leasing an empty hole."

Gabe flared, "He did not. I decided on my own, after Neville leased your northeastern claims to that Aloysius Everard character."

Jessie sat bolt upright. "To who?"

"Aw, some professor of mineralogy from back East," Gabe replied, still scowling at Mastleg Thistle. "And if Everard has the brains to spot a hot prospect, I durn well have the brains to follow his lead."

Jessie leaned forward intensely. "What's he look like?"

"Everard?" Gabe shrugged. "I dunno. I've never met him."

"Aye, Everard's a recluse. Neville drew the lease, and as long as Everard pays him my rent, I'll respect his privacy."

Returning, Unity set the table. When she was serving the stew, Mastleg chuckled smugly. "I daren't get too chummy. The Monteplata never had high-grade ore, but if a young lubber and a barmy scientist want to prove different, I'll take their money—just not their complaints."

After the meal, Jessie said, "We'd best head back to Virginia City now. The lawyer's not much, but he's worth a try."

Unity declared that she wished to go, and Gabe asked to ride along too. "I need supplies, but I'd rather not risk it alone just yet."

"It's a hot, dusty trip," Mastleg complained, "so I might as well make it in company. I'm nigh out of airtights, and need to jaw with Neville about makin' sure Noah can't weasel out of his lease."

"Thistle, checking leases is not what you need most to do," Unity objected. "You should be getting ready for a gun ruckus."

"Let 'em come, m' lass. I'd sure admire t' have 'em try it."

"I suppose you'll lick Gabe's dad and brothers and crew all by your lonesome." Unity frowned disgustedly. "Lick, hell."

Mastleg lit the cigarette he'd started to roll before lunch, snatched up his rifle, and thumped outside. Gabe and Ki banked the cookstove fire, then went out and found Mastleg in a lean-to shed, and helped him hitch a choleric walleyed mule to a rickety narrow-gauge Democrat wagon. He climbed up and stayed there, arguing with the mule.

Shortly they left for Virginia City. Gabe led this time, followed by Ki, Jessie, and Unity, the wagon tagging last. Hoof-tossed dust enveloped the wagon, whose wheels wobbled loudly on worn, dry hubs, but Mastleg kept pace with a vengeance. He handled the traces with stinging hands, kicked the boards with his pegleg just to aggravate the mule, and prodded those ahead into a more rapid clip.

The miles fell behind. They crossed the serrated canyons and ridges, forded Dishwater Creek, and wound through the range of low hills into the broad pass. As the pass began to funnel toward the shadowy gorge, Ki felt a swiftly increasing uneasiness.

He trusted his intuition, honed sharp by training and experience. He shifted his gaze from the flanking slopes to the rubbled floor of the pass, but failed to glimpse anything wrong. He still felt compelled to

75

trot up even with Gabe, and point to the .44 Spencer carbine in Gabe's saddle boot.

"Check the magazine and then keep your hand on the stock," he said. "We're riding into trouble."

Gabe looked at him with a puzzled expression, but did as he'd been told.

Reining in, Ki waited for Jessie to catch up, studying the trail ahead as he did so. It curved through a ragged copse of spruce and scrub oak that rose from tangled underbrush and wide, jagged boulders. There was a sort of haze, an ominous, muffled murkiness to the air.

Jessie drew alongside. "What's wrong?" she asked.

Barely were the words out of her mouth when a volley of gunfire cut through the mist. Bullets ripped by mere inches away, snapping off a branch overhead. There was an ugle *splat!* as Jessie's bay mare took a slug, shuddered once, faltered, and started to fall. Jessie flung herself clear as the animal went down, thrashing and whinnying.

"Off the trail!" Ki shouted. "Get off and down!"

More guns were opening fire now, as they plunged for concealment. With the exception of Mastleg, whose panicked mule was plowing him and his flimsy wagon deeper into the woods, they dove behind the closest possible shelter, a rampart of loose boulders enclosing a small rocky depression. Dismounting, grabbing weapons and extra ammo and fanning out, they hugged their stone cover while salvos of lead poured in, ripping undergrowth, slashing trees, and ricocheting off rocks.

Mastleg appeared, bounding from where his mule had rammed to a halt in a briar thicket. Hurdling awkwardly over brush and weaving through the gauntlet of bullets, he scrambled up beside Jessica, with the Peabody in his right hand and a cannister of cartridges in his left.

"Saw 'em, I saw 'em," he panted, daubing his

thorn-scratched face. "Gawd, two dozen or more, some in them Posse Comitatus hoods, one gang drubbing the trail, and another roughin' straight for us."

Jessie nodded. "We're set, whatever direction they hit us from."

"Set for good, if they hit more of our horses," Ki countered. "We're lucky any are still alive. We've got to take them somewhere safer."

As he spoke, Ki was acting on his suggestion, moving swiftly to collect the three remaining horses. Gathering the reins, Ki led the horses out between the boulders and ran them back the way Mastleg had come. Within minutes he located the wagon and mule. The animal was placidly munching thistle blooms in a reasonably hidden pocket of briars and brambles. He tethered the horses and mule securely and started to return—then changed his mind.

Instead, Ki angled toward the trail. Sprinting in a low crouch, he ignored the gunfire that seared from the brush and from farther up the trail, and concentrated on picking a suitable tree. Long before reaching it, he chose a dense box alder that slightly overhung the trail. He paused at its base for a moment while he drew his short curved *tanto* from its waistband sheath. Then, holding the blade between his teeth, he shinnied up the alder's trunk with the agility of a monkey. When he sensed that he was just high enough to be camouflaged by the foliage, he squatted silently in a fork and waited.

Inside the ring of boulders, Jessie began to wonder what was delaying Ki. Mastleg was quietly testing different positions for his rifle. Gabe, his carbine and reloads already arranged, didn't have enough to occupy him and was nervously chattering, "We oughta be able to stop 'em, if we don't get rattled and go scatterin' our shots." And Unity was resting, outwardly calm, though she kept repeating grimly, "Hit a man if you can; if you can't hit a man, hit his horse."

77

Unity left off reciting and checked her Winchester. It barked in unison with the Peabody that Mastleg had lined on the ten or twelve hooded riders, who were charging up the trail in plain sight and easy range.

A grunt of satisfaction told that Mastleg had gotten his man. Unity had winged hers; he was leaning limply in his saddle, so she levered again and struck down his horse, crushing him underneath it as it rolled, kicking up a dust cloud in its death throes. Jessie and Gabe rushed over to help, though Jessica's .38 was rendered ineffective by the distance, and Gabe missed his first shot, his aim disrupted by the dust.

By now the balance of riders were slowing hastily, wrenching their horses aside to keep them from stumbling over bodies as they veered toward the makeshift barricade. Another fusillade met their advance, Mastleg hitting his target again. Gabe let out a whoop when his second shot dumped a rider from the saddle. Jessie managed to cripple a horse, which crumpled abruptly on its forelegs, catapulting its rider into the path of the others. The attack began to falter, the riders milling about in a tight clump, stirring up still more billowing dust.

It was Ki, however, who shattered the attack.

One rider, apparently trying to make an end run, swerved in so close that he brushed the trunk of the box alder. Carefully timing his release, Ki fell onto the horse's rump as it galloped beneath his branch, landing with his upper legs splayed for sitting, his calves and heels instantly squeezing inward to hold his seat. His hands were already in motion, his left clamping over the rider's hooded head, fingers hooking into eye sockets to give him leverage. He jerked the rider's head backwards, while his right hand passed the *tanto*'s blade across the abruptly exposed throat, before the rider even knew he was there.

One slash, through the jugular and the windpipe. Then Ki pushed the man's head forward to keep the blood from fountaining, switched his knife to his left hand, and reached with his now empty right hand to snatch the man's carbine from his lifeless fingers before it could drop.

The horse was still galloping, but was becoming spooked by the sudden weighty turmoil and the scent of fresh blood. It turned white-eyed as Ki knocked the dead rider out of the saddle. The man tumbled limply, his head hinging unnaturally and spewing gouts of crimson. Sliding into the saddle and grasping the reins, Ki fought the horse's hysteria for a few moments, finally regaining control and sending the horse in headlong flight back toward the oncoming riders.

Before the startled Posse could recover and respond, Ki triggered, levered, and triggered again. Two riders toppled from their saddles with gaping holes in their chests.

The four defenders behind the boulders backed Ki's counterattack with spirited shooting of their own. The Posse wavered, unable to withstand the crossfire boring into the ranks, then broke, scattering in retreat.

Ki slewed the horse around and sped for the boulders. Joining the others, he said, "One gang down, for a while at least, till they regroup."

"Good, we've earned a breather," Jessie sighed.

"Aye, but not yet," Mastleg growled, squinting through the crevice where his rifle was propped. "The other gang's bellyin' up afoot, skulkin' in the brush and behind trees, Injun-style. I'd wager they're aimin' to work on us from long range for a spell."

Gabe flashed Jessie an ironic smile. "Well, there's your breather. We'll lay low and let 'em whang away till they get tired."

"Not a bad idea," Jessie replied, and Unity nodded, adding, "I agree. Don't nobody risk fighting back 'less they attack again."

Less than five minutes later the second gang opened fire. Their siege soon proved fully as savage as the previous assault, and far more effective in that they stayed safely concealed while concentrating their volleys into the boulders.

The defenders stuck tight, saving their ammunition and presenting no targets. Yet they had precious little protection from the chance shots and ricochets that kept cycloning around the rocks, and it was simply a matter of time and odds before one or more would be hit.

Suddenly Gabe, lying on hip and elbow, sucked in his breath with a sharp hiss. Wincing, he clutched his left leg, rolling over on his back to frown up at Unity, who had leaped to bend anxiously over him.

"It's nothing, just a scratch. But of all the bum luck!"

"Let me see," she insisted, tugging at his boot.

Reluctantly, Gabe let Unity help him take off his boot and raise his trouser leg. His wound was more than a scratch but less than a serious injury, the stray bullet having burned a welt across the side of his shinbone and gouged a deep furrow in his fleshy calf. The shin hurt more, but the furrow was bleeding profusely. Using Gabe's tan shirt and his hunting knife, Unity began fashioning flannel bandages.

Meanwhile, Ki was snaking outside the boulders, not content to remain hidden and on the defensive. He crept on knees and forearms to a shallow knoll clustered with tall brush. From a vantage point cloaked by the brush, he surveyed the area.

The chronic firing had no pattern and was spread haphazardly through the timber and undergrowth, so it took Ki a while to pinpoint the gunners. By then, bullets were pelting down from the trees and the nearby cliff face, indicating that some ambitious attackers had climbed to gain elevation and a clear shot into the stone enclosure. That was bad enough—but when, moments later, Ki started noticing things much closer in, he abruptly slipped out from the brush, and slithered on his stomach down the knoll and across to the boulders.

Crawling in, he called for attention and then reported, "They've regrouped. Except for those who are pinning us down, both gangs have combined into one big crew—a raiding crew—and it's coming anytime."

Mastleg caught up his rifle, snarling throatily, "Let 'em come, damn 'em. They won't be so many of 'em after a bit."

Come they did, the Posse attacking viciously, confident that they'd ultimately win by attrition. Features twisted in a vicious snarl, a hoodless rider stormed in with a heavy Colt Dragoon in his fist, but Gabe's Spencer took him out. A slug from Unity's carbine slammed another man back off his horse. Mastleg looked utterly dispassionate as he watched one target fold, and searched for the next live one he could add to the growing dead.

Jessie continued to use her pistol, swinging its smoking muzzle to meet the blast of another revolver, just as it sent a slug spanging off a rock less than a foot from her. Not even blinking, she triggered her pistol at the man looming behind the one just fallen.

Strangely, in this long moment of lancing gunflame and hammering bullets, Jessie felt calm and acutely aware of everything at once. She saw Ki grinning his thin metallic grin; he was in his element here, a professional doing his job. Mastleg was grim and silent, and Gabe's teeth were bared in a carnal grimace. And Unity, handling her carbine with smooth dispatch, had an ashen-faced expression, obviously too shocked and terrified to do anything except fight like a demon.

And then Jessie glimpsed Mastleg collapsing suddenly, a red splotch spreading swiftly above his belt. Springing to him, she dragged him to a more sheltered spot. Mastleg smiled wanly and struggled to sit up. "Gutshot . . . won't last long . . . fetch me my rifle and some cartridges, matey, and get back to the cannon deck."

Jessie propped his Peabody and cannister case next to him, then stuffed some of Gabe's leftover bandages against the wound and clasped Mastleg's weakening hand over it. He nodded, closing his eyes. Her face as rigid as carved granite, Jessie turned away to reload her pistol and resume the slaughter.

Lead was buzzing and snapping among the boulders, and the rocky depression was becoming enveloped in an acrid smoke cloud.

Yet it wasn't a battle that could last. Although more numerous than before, the Posse was exposed to entrenched defenders. They needed a swift assault to win, but instead they were stalling again, riders milling uncertainly while their companions were knocked from saddles as if cuffed by a mighty unseen hand. Others locked arms around their horses' necks to keep from falling. One swayed upright, his horse angling almost to the trail before he dropped off.

Unity hastened from Mastleg to Ki, her face wan. "Here, we use the same caliber, so I'll split the last of my shells with you," she offered. "And Thistle is awfully sick."

Ki saw that Mastleg seemed to have wilted, his head nodding forward, his hands flaccid in his bloodied lap. A gentle movement of his blood-soaked blazer showed that Mastleg was still breathing, but he was beyond being sick. He was dead, and just didn't know it.

"Thanks for the rounds, Unity," Ki responded. "It's kind of hard now, but your stepfather will get tended to as soon as possible."

Unity nodded and turned away. Ki was watching her, shaking his own head sadly, when a change in the fighting struck him suddenly.

No question about it, the firing was subsiding, first around the boulders, then widening slowly across the

82

thickets and groves, gradually silencing even the long barrels up on the cliff face.

Ki strode out of the boulders and strained his powder-stung eyes through the sulfurous gunsmoke. He was still unable to see any live attackers, but he was surrounded by an appalling carnage of human and animal corpses. Then, faintly, from beyond the screen of brush and trees, he heard the drumming of many hooves receding to the east, into remote country.

He turned and went back into the boulders to attend to Mastleg, though he knew it was probably a mistake to allow Unity hope by implying through his actions that there was anything to be done for her stepfather beyond digging him a grave. But it didn't seem right just now to slap her with the truth.

"They'd better not rush us again," Jessie said, falling in beside him. "I've only got two bullets left, and I don't think anybody else is much better off."

Ki nodded, exhaling heavily. "Yes, Jessie, it was too close for my liking, but I don't think they'll come after us again right now."

Gabe limped up and added, "It was a genuine squeaker, all right. For a while I thought them vigilantes was gonna run right over us for sure."

Coming to Mastleg's side, they hunkered down next to him. He was lying back, his head cradled in Unity's arms, his breathing painful and raspy.

"I reckon that'll hold 'em on their tether," he said in a bubbling whisper. "We licked 'em good an' proper, didn't we?" Then he let out a long, shuddering breath and lay still, staring sightlessly upward.

Gabe handed Mastleg's rifle to Ki, then stooped to help Unity close Mastleg's eyes and stretch him out. When she rose, he patted her trim shoulder and said hoarsely, "Chin up, gal."

She said, "We aren't burying him here."

"No, we couldn't stay here that long, anyway. If that bunch gets some courage back, things could go bad very fast." Ki turned and started toward the wagon. "We'll take him into town."

"What about all them other bodies?" Gabe called.

Before Ki could reply, Unity said in a cold, brittle voice, "Leave them for the vultures, Gabe, that's what we'll do—if the vultures will have them."

★

Chapter 8

They laid out Mastleg in the wagon bed.

Wrestling the ribbons and the cranky mule, Ki started the wagon toward Virginia City. Gabe and Jessie, on Ki's bay mare, fell in ahead of the dust-spuming wheels. Unity had tied her pinto to the tail-gate and now rode, mute and unsmiling, on the seat alongside Ki.

More than ever, Ki wondered at Unity's steady reserve. She wasn't outwardly grieving, and he doubted that she'd loved Mastleg as she had her father. Yet obviously she'd been fond of him, caring enough to make this point of accompanying his body in the wagon. Once again, Ki sensed that beneath her composure lay a warmth of spirit, smoldering like the coals of a banked forge.

Ah, lucky Gabe, who alone seemed to have a chance of igniting her affections. Not that Ki felt jealous; he'd taken a liking to the rambunctious young miner. And as conversation drifted back to the wagon, it was evident that Jessie also approved, attracted as she was by Gabe's pleasant personality and virile appearance.

Everyone was tense, distressed by the ambush and wary of another. Yet the trip proved uneventful, and they reached Virginia City as the sun descended into late afternoon. They paused at the marshal's office, but Tilden and his deputy were out somewhere and the door was locked. They moved on, then, to the Divine Hands Funeral Parlor, which was sandwiched incongruously between a ribald saloon and a piano-clanging dance hall.

Dismounting, Gabe said, "Arrangin' things may take a while."

"In that case, Jessie and I might as well return my horse," Ki replied as he climbed from the wagon. "We'll meet you back here."

"No, let's meet at the lawyer's," Jessie countered firmly. "That is, if Unity feels up to having a little talk with him."

Unity nodded, pale and tight-lipped. Gabe gave directions to Chester Neville's law office, then strode into the funeral parlor to get some "divine hands" to help move Mastleg's body. Jessie handed Ki the reins and said, "Here. I want to make a quick stop at the hotel."

"Flynn won't be happy without you along to explain what happened to your horse," Ki predicted.

"I couldn't care less," Jessie replied. She meant it, her mind already focused on what she might learn back in her hotel room.

She hastened along the street, where a steady stream of men flowed around her with their hobnailed boots drumming the boardwalks. Entering the Palace and going straight to her room, she locked the door and removed a small black leather-bound notebook from her luggage. She seated herself by the window for light, and began studying the book's pages, searching for a particular entry.

The book was a copy of her father's original ledger,

which she kept under lock and key at the Circle Star Ranch, her Texas home. The original was old, worn, and too valuable to travel with, dating from when Alex Starbuck had started compiling lists of every businessman, lawman, politician, and outright crook involved with the cartel. Since his death, Jessie had continued updating the information, gathering data through personal experience and from reports submitted by Starbuck operatives throughout the country and the world.

She found nothing under the name Chester Neville, but wasn't surprised; so far there was nothing suspicious about the lawyer, and even if there was, aliases were not uncommon. Under Aloysius Everard, however, was the short entry she'd thought she recalled when Gabe had inadvertently dropped the name during his flare-up at Mastleg.

> *EVERARD, Xavier Aloysius, b. Aug. 19, 1834, Patterson, New Jersey. 5' 10", well built flashy dresser, sometimes wears well-trimmed mustache. 3 yrs Yale Univ., geol. major, expelled for lewdness. Geol. bkgrnd used in swindles. May 2, 1857, arrested & escaped, Atlanta, Georgia (cf. Diamond Exch. Hoax). Sept.-Oct. 1861, similar conv., Leadville, Colo. (cf. Pandora Gold Mines), bribed presiding judge. Dec. 1869, stock swindle, Sebastian, Mont. (cf. Copper Mountain Syndicate), arrested, tried, sentenced to 10 yrs. Died Feb. 10, 1876, buried Deer Lodge Penitentiary.*

Now, finally, she had a confirmed link between the cartel and something other than Unity's torn photo—her father's worthless mining property, by the smell of it. But the link was four years dead.

Returning the notebook to her luggage, Jessie left the Palace and hurried to the corner of C and Stanton streets, where the others were waiting outside a large block building identified by a weathered sign that read FIRST NEVADA BANK & TRUST. An upper window carried a legend in gilt letters on its grimy panes: CHESTER B. NEVILLE, ATTORNEY-AT-LAW.

"Your horse was a prize racing brood mare, judging by what Flynn made me pay," Ki informed her, as the four wedged past speculators who jammed around the bank's bulletin board of mine stock quotations.

While they were mounting the lobby staircase to the upper floor, Unity explained, "The coroner can't get to certifying until late tomorrow, so that's when Thistle will have his send-off. No hearse, no flowers, no mourning. Just us and a pine board box."

"Do me a favor," Jessie asked Unity, as Gabe knocked on an oak door bearing the lawyer's name. "Get Neville talking about any old thing, then work around to Professor Everard and his mine claim."

The door opened to reveal a hawk-nosed, furrow-cheeked man about fifty, silken hair turning a distinguished gray, in crisp white shirtsleeves. A green eyeshade cowled his high, lined forehead.

"Gabe, and Miss Balsam, how nice," he greeted them in a cordial Carolina drawl. "Is this purely social, or may I serve y'all?"

Unity answered, politely yet coolly, "You handled my stepfather's business, so I suppose you'll represent his estate."

"His estate? Merciful heavens! Come in, come in!"

As they stepped inside, Neville began to quickly group chairs at his desk. Glancing about, Jessie surmised that he'd taken over Lou Heiligman's office along with his practice; the walls were covered with faded paper and pictures of barristers from bygone eras, and the previous attorney's name was embossed on the spines of the volumes of Blackstone and the Nevada statutes that filled the bookcases.

"Do I understand that Mr. Thistle has passed away?" Neville asked as he finished moving the chairs. "His health? An accident?"

Ignoring his questions, Unity sat down and said, "Mr. Neville, let me introduce Miss Starbuck and Mr. Ki, close friends of mine."

"Miss Starbuck?" Neville unhooked his suit jacket from a nearby coat rack, and apologized to Jessica as he slipped it on. "Please excuse my rude *deshabille,*" he murmured, doffing his eyeshade. "This is an unexpected honor, to meet a queen of industry such as yourself."

"The pleasure's mine," she replied, stifling an urge to gag. She loathed flattery, even from a man whose eyes were as honest as any she'd ever seen—maybe a little *too* honest—and especially when his formality was absurd, such as now, when they were all far more casually dressed, and rumpled and dirty besides. All right, so Neville might be an unctuous shyster, she thought, but he was *not* Aloysius Everard, as she'd slimly hoped he might, just might, turn out to be.

"We were together," Unity continued, "when Thistle was shot."

"Gunned down? And y'all witnessed it? Lord, who did it?"

Gabe answered venomously, "The Posse Comitatus. They jumped us while we was headin' to town, and plugged Mastleg in the scuffle."

"My most heartfelt condolences," Neville offered, settling in his desk chair. "Have you notified Marshal Tilden of this tragedy?"

"He was out when we tried to." Unity sighed, shrugging. "Not much he can do; he can't even keep up with the killings here in town."

"No lawman could, Miss Balsam. But until he and the coroner file their official reports, my hands are tied. Mr. Thistle's affairs must remain confidential, and his estate closed preparatory to probate."

Unity bridled. "My mother left no will, meaning in this state that Thistle and I were joint heirs to the only estate then or now, the Monteplata. It didn't produce enough to share, and I didn't want to fool

89

with it. But letting Thistle run both halves doesn't make me lose part ownership. Read your Nevada law books. Whether he's alive or dead, I can demand a check of my interests anytime I choose."

"Yesss...you'd be within your rights." Nodding thoughtfully, Neville twisted in his chair, dialed the combination of the standup safe behind his desk, edged open its laminated iron door, and drew out a manila accordion folder. Swiveling frontward to give Unity the folder, he added genially, "If you have questions, please ask me."

"I will," Unity said, scanning the contents: balance sheets, debit vouchers, billing invoices, schedules and supplemental analyses, and the lease agreements. She gave a few papers to Gabe and the leases to Jessie, while she concentrated on the profit-and-loss statements.

Neville, realizing belatedly that Unity was no dunce, grew less gracious. "You'll find my accounts are in order," he said stiffly. "Lou Heiligman's records are in there too, and just go to show that, as you admitted, the Monteplata never earned a sou. To put it bluntly, the only way your stepfather could pay expenses was by leasing some of the claims, initially to Dr. Everard and then to Gabe here—a fine, hearty lad who's going places, mark my word."

At last the conversation had hit upon Jessie's main concern. "Why would a mineral expert lease a played-out mine from you, Mr. Neville?"

The lawyer hesitated as though resisting, then spread his palms on the desktop. "Very well, but I must have your pledge of secrecy. Everard's doctorate is in geological engineering, which must be something impressive; it got him hired by an eastern syndicate figuring on rising ore prices. Anyway, he came to explore the Monteplata for potential revival, then leased the northeast slope to survey in detail, virtually convinced that some old veins there are just dead offshoots from very deep, rich lodes. Of course, we've kept this quiet to avoid a rush."

"And diverted curiosity by bandying it about that Everard's a crackpot hermit," Jessie declared. "Is he actually out there poking around?"

"Far as I know. Last time we met, Everard told me he's staying in camp until his syndicate responds to the tests he's submitted."

"What's he really like? What's he look like?"

"I'm six foot . . ." Neville paused again, tenting his fingers. "I'd estimate Everard's a bit shorter and younger than me. Always wears clean britches and shirts, and a cream-colored Stetson. Stubby mustache, and I guess he's handsome, in a rather sly sort of manner."

"You don't trust him?"

"I've no reason not to," Neville retorted, testy from Jessie's pressuring. "I've negotiated and maintained all contracts as best I could, and I assure you, Everard's always prompt and cooperative. But I'll cancel his lease and evict him if Miss Balsam orders me to."

Unity gave a cynical laugh. "I couldn't afford to. No, you're managing fine," she said, handing the folder back to Neville. She glanced at Jessie then, asking, "Anything else we need to discuss?"

Slowly Jessie shook her head, stifling her excitement.

Unity hesitated, puzzled; Jessie looked as though she wasn't entirely convinced and might change her mind. When Jessie didn't, Unity eyed Gabe and Ki, who sat attentive yet silent, and then rose.

"Well, we've learned what we can, I imagine, and I'll be late for work at this rate," she said, regarding Neville again. "Thanks."

"Stay in touch, m'dear." Beaming effusively, Neville accompanied the four to his door. "And the good Lord be with y'all, y'hear?"

When they reached the bank lobby and were angling toward the street exit, Jessie asked Unity, "What do you think of Neville?"

"Oozes sheep dip, but his figures don't lie." She made a faint smile that had no mirth to it. "He's not much of a lawyer, though. I made up that stuff about Nevada law, and he never tumbled to it."

Just then Marshal Tilden opened the street door, saw them, and held it open until they'd filed outside. "I was looking for you," he growled, grim-visaged.

"I heard. I'm awful sorry, Unity."

Unity faced him, wordless, with a condemning expression.

"Sorry I was out, too," Tilden tried again. "Now the undertaker said you'd told him it was the Posse that did in poor Mastleg."

"Yeah, they bushwhacked us next to the gorge, about halfway 'tween Mastleg's cabin and town," Gabe explained. "A whole passel of 'em. Should be a plain mess of prints to track 'em by."

"I'll get on it, but don't post high hopes. Them killers scatter in the hills long before they take roost, and it'd need a company of Indian scouts to flush 'em out, not just one lone marshal."

Ki asked, "Any ideas who they are?"

"Wish I had. The leader, whoever he is, keeps a mighty low profile and spends scads of money. Some men buy cheap, others come high, but there're always plenty of strangers here who'll sell at some price."

Jessie frowned. "Not even one's been caught?"

"Not in shape to talk," Tilden conceded sadly. "I'd sure like to. I'd like to break through their hooded anonymity and smash 'em."

"And lynch 'em, too," Unity lashed out caustically. "You'd like to hang 'em high, on the spot!"

She pivoted and strode away. Gabe dashed after her, but she ignored him, vanishing into the crowds, heading toward the Silverado Club.

Tilden stood stone-still for a moment, then said gloomily, "I don't blame her. As a young'un, she had blind faith in her dad and absolute trust in the law. When Enoch robbed, he betrayed her, and when he was strung up, she felt the law had betrayed her too."

"Had it?" Jessie asked. "Did you help lynch him?"

"Ma'am, I was outnumbered and powerless, but Unity's convinced I could've stopped the hanging and saved him. I did fail her, though, later, when I lost the guts to arrest the lynchers."

"Hard lessons are to be learned, not relived," Ki advised, and shifted topics before Tilden brooded himself into a funk. "I understand you've got a born tracker for a nephew. Why not use him, enlist the townsmen, and fight the Posse the same way you did back then?"

Tilden's expression soured. "First, my nephew died in that fight. Second, I learned my lesson and will never lead a pack of human wolves again." He moved to go, turning to add, "I won't bother warning you to stay clean, 'cause there's enough grief brewing to slather us all. It's just such a shame the good ones always wind up corpses."

They watched the marshal stomp off around a corner, and then Jessie said, "Come on, Ki, the other way, to the telegraph office. I've got more bits to the puzzle, but they don't seem to fit, either."

They began heading in the opposite direction, toward the train depot. In low tones, Jessie recounted Everard's entries in her notebook and Neville's matching thumbnail description of him, and ended by suggesting, "Everard's a con artist, and he might've rigged a phony death so he could escape prison without being missed."

"Perhaps," Ki allowed, "but most authorities are wise to deceptions, particularly fake burials. In any case, the quick and sure solution is to go and see who's at Everard's claim." He paused to gaze at the livid sunset. "Too late today, though. It's too far to ride before nightfall, and would be impossible to locate after dark."

"Stop dawdling, or it'll be too late to send my cables."

Ki nodded, his glance scanning the street as they started to walk again. His swift eyes fixed on a man coming out of the bank building behind him. It needed no special examination to identify him; Chester Neville stood resplendent beside the lobby door, leaning lightly against the wall as he scrutinized the direction away from Ki.

Instantly, before Neville could turn and see them, Ki grabbed Jessie's arm and steered her into a deepset entryway. Startled, her first reaction was to snap, "What in hell!" Then she closed her mouth, seeing Ki peer cautiously around the entryway, and her second thought was that he'd spotted another ambusher.

Ki stepped out then, craning his neck to view farther. "Our lawyer friend is going someplace, furtive as a fox in a barnyard. I think I'll find out where and why." He grinned fleetingly at Jessie. "When you send your wires, toss in a few for Neville. Who knows?"

Then he was gone, swallowed by the evening traffic. Jessie waited a few minutes, then continued on to the telegraph office.

The crimson skyline flamed the crests above Virginia City, leaving by contrast an ashen mauve shadow down within the streets. The pallid dimness subdued the squalor more than it concealed it, but Ki was grateful even for this. It made it easier to trail Neville.

The lawyer walked with feline suppleness, and though he didn't take any evasive action, he frequently stopped to check behind him, as if he sensed that someone was following him. Ki stayed out of his sight, Neville's silk top hat acting as a beacon for Ki, twenty yards behind. By the time Neville turned left off Idaho Street, Ki realized they were heading down into the scruffier part of town, and he felt a strange, intuitive hunch that he was being led to the Silverado.

Why not? Might as well make it four "coincidences."

Approaching the club, Ki let his glance drift ahead of Neville. Tied at a nearby hitch rail, a line-backed grulla caught his eye; it looked familiar, and suddenly he knew why. It was the horse ridden by that lanky vigilante who'd done all the talking at Gabe's lynching bee.

Well, now. Make it five "coincidences."

The pirate doorman opened the door for Neville. Blue smoke billowed out from the entrance; the air reeked with sweat, cheap perfume, and cheaper whiskey, and quivered with shouts and laughter from the drunken customers. The door closed behind Neville.

Ki quickened his pace, and was almost to the doorman when abruptly the door slammed open from inside. Gabe barged outside, hauling Unity along by her wrist. He thrust her over to the side of the entrance opposite the doorman, gripping her tightly, talking low and passionately, only odd words and phrases rising above the noise.

Ki heard him say, "You fancy him . . . I won't let you . . . half Oriental . . ." He veered hastily into the alleyway siding the club. This wasn't a coincidence, this was a pain in the ass, stupidly delaying him.

Gabe's voice rose again—"Flirting with Ki . . . !" —then dropped back to garbled snippets. And Ki decided that remaining here was preferable to walking past them. Their spat involved him, and sounded asinine enough to erupt into a fight if given temptation.

Unity was too angry to keep her tone down. "Shame on you, Gabriel! You're just jealous of Ki because— er, that is, because—"

"Why?" Gabe demanded. "I know why you think I'm jealous. You think I'm jealous 'cause I've the right to be. And I have!"

"You don't, never did! In your conceit, you assumed I'd marry you. I admit I might've done so, just wandered along and done so, if you hadn't acted as you have tonight. But as things are now—!"

There was a sharp, resounding smack, such as might be made by a palm striking a cheek, and Gabe yelled, "Do what you damn well want to! See if I care!" Then there was only the hubbub from inside the Silverado.

Ki waited a few seconds, then came out of the alley. Gabe and Unity were gone, and that was a relief; Ki didn't want to hurt them.

The pirate doorman opened the door, and Ki stepped inside.

As Ki had feared, Neville was no longer there.

★

Chapter 9

Jessie, arriving at the depot's telegraph office, composed an innocent-sounding wire to the Circle Star Ranch. The telegrapher was amazed by its expensive length, but would have been even more astounded if he'd been able to read it correctly.

Jessie's code was sophisticated and confidential, known only by herself and Ki, and a few trusted employees of the Starbuck organization. Once they received and deciphered her message, they'd launch into an extensive research of Aloysius Everard, with emphasis on his last swindle—the Copper Mountain Syndicate—his accomplices, prison history, and death. Jessie also requested information on the old train robbery and on Chester Neville, though she doubted anything important would turn up that she didn't already know. Replies were needed as soon as possible, sent in care of the Palace Hotel.

After paying the Overland Telegraph clerk, Jessie returned to the hotel to see if Ki was back with any interesting news. He was not, but a wax-sealed note was waiting for her at the front desk. The note was on linen bond, imprinted with Neville's name and address, and written in his crabbed hand and courtly style.

Dear Miss Starbuck,
Please pardon my intrusion, but I must beg a short visit with you this evening. Please call at my home any time after seven o'clock. I assure you I would not impose upon your valuable time if it were not for the grave urgency of the subject at hand.

Your obedient servant,
Chester B. Neville, Esq.

Jessie took the note to her room, freshened up, and sat for some moments in thoughtful silence. Then she got up with sudden decision, and went to the lobby to ask directions to Neville's home.

The lawyer lived near Millionaire's Row, in a fine townhouse of white clapboard and dark stone. A butler in a swallowtail coat answered the door, and ushered Jessie along a parquet-tiled hallway to an inner parlor, which was windowless, lined with bookshelves, and furnished with tufted velvet upholstery.

Neville rose from a wingback chair. "So good of you to come."

"I couldn't refuse a grave urgency," Jessie replied.

Meanwhile, the butler was filling two snifters with cognac. He set them and the bottle on a table, and left. The table was between two facing chairs, and Neville went to one side, raised the closer glass, and offered, "To our better acquaintance."

"I'll drink to that," Jessie agreed calmly.

Sipping, Neville ambled toward the door. "Apparently, Miss Starbuck—may I call you Jessica?—apparently, Jessica, you're firm friends with Unity and Gabe." He reclosed the door and strolled back, his eyes taking their slow, bold fill of her. "Am I wrong to assume you'd go to some lengths to catch Mr. Thistle's murderers?"

"I would, willingly. Do you know who they are?"

"I've a theory, but no proof. Except this." Opening a drawer of the table, he drew out a piece of wrapping paper with writing on it, and handed it to Jessie. "I found it today, nailed to my door."

Jessie read it aloud. "'Neville, we could have burned you out, and next time we will. Take our advice and stick to your legals, and stop nosing where you don't belong.'" Below the smeared block letters were the numerals 3-7-77 and a crudely drawn death's head. "The Posse killed Mastleg, but why would they want to threaten you?" Jessie asked after considering the note for a moment.

"Well, we were connected in that Mr. Thistle owned the Monteplata, and I've been the attorney for it. The Monteplata's only fame is that it's the scene of the great bullion disappearance, which in turn has made it the focus of treasure hunters."

She returned the paper. "Fine, but this is hardly proof."

"No? Look, for all its crude lettering, not one word is misspelled, and the language is that of an educated man," he declared, tucking the paper away. "Like a mineralogy expert."

She straightened. "Aloysius Everard?"

"Jessie, I wager you've got half the men in Nevada panting after you." Neville said it with studied careless bantering, yet his deepset eyes watched for any slight response in her expression.

Guilelessly she asked, "Why would he want to kill you?"

"Everard's frantically searching for the bullion. It doesn't exist. It's too clumsy to hide well, and anywhere the robbers might've dumped it has been scoured clean for years. No, it was located long ago and quietly removed, but Everard is afraid that because we control

99

the property, we'll spy on him and evict him if he ever finds any."

"I see. We need more proof, though."

"If there's evidence, it's probably with Everard. But he'd suspect me. Would you visit him, you and your gentleman friend?"

"I'll ask him," Jessie hedged, stifling a laugh. "We've no idea where Everard's claim is, though, or how to ride there."

"Actually, he's not at his digs right now, but he told me where he proposed to camp." Neville drew paper and a pencil from the drawer, and began to draw a map. Finally he explained the lines: "Here's the trail to Mr. Thistle's, and here's the cutoff you take. Here, at the northeast end, is a canyon, and here's one a couple of miles south of it. The first leads past the slope where Everard has his main digs. But you don't take that one, understand?"

Jessie nodded, feeling his eyes undressing her again.

"Take the second canyon, this one to the south, and go due east for five or six miles until it broadens into a meadowland. That's where Everard should be camping. Don't do anything risky, just try to stick around awhile and pick up whatever you can."

Jessie rose as Neville came around the table to hand her the drawing. "Thank you," she said. "Now if you'll excuse me—"

"Not yet. When was the last time you had a man, Jessica?"

She tensed. "I want to get an early start, so I—"

"I knew it, I knew it. I can always tell." His voice was suave, and his arm was around her shoulders. "You're not in tune with nature, m'dear. The whites of your eyes are not very clear."

"I'm sure nature is grateful for your diagnosis," she snapped, "but I am not." She pulled away from him, alarmed by a sudden savage glint in Neville's eyes.

It was only there for a fraction of a moment, then

Neville laughed. "Late bloomers are such fun. Don't let that temper of yours cheat you of a rewarding experience."

Furious, she said, "It would be easy to hate you."

His lunge caught her unprepared. Wheeling, she tried to duck away, but he had her by both wrists and she was unable to prevent him from drawing her pistol and tossing it across the room, then locking her in his arms. She strained backward, pushing at his chest. "Let go!" she panted. "Stop it!"

He was surprisingly strong, with large hands and long fingers, and he held her without much effort. He tried to kiss her, and she bent her head, her mouth tight and her lips clenched. "If you won't give me kisses," he said with a hard-breathing grin, "I'll have to steal them." He tried again, and she managed to free an arm. She struck him a stinging slap across the face with her open palm.

His recoil gave her an opportunity, and she wrenched herself out of his grasp and bolted for the door. He overtook her just as she discovered the door was locked—so *that* was what he'd done when he'd strolled to the door!—and pinned her against the door with his body.

Jessie gasped for air, her eyes narrowing and then widening as he slid a hand up her flank. "You filthy beast!" she hissed.

He had her wrists firmly grasped in one hand, and he ran the other hand across her breasts, trying to unbutton her blouse. As she attempted to twist away, there was a sharp ripping noise, and her blouse seemed to tear apart at the seams, suddenly exposing her heaving unbound breasts.

Desperately she backed against the door and kicked at his shins. Neville merely shifted a pace backward and held her straight-armed against the door. But her legs were long and she hammered him sufficiently to make him wince. There was no sign of surrender or tears in her, but only a wildness born of fury and the passionate urge to kill him if possible.

When he began to fondle her right breast, his hold relaxed for a second and she sank her teeth into his forearm. He yelled with unexpected pain, but countered instantly with the flat of his hand across her mouth. She tried to thrust evasively, at least long enough for her to grab her derringer hidden behind her belt buckle, but he seized her around the waist and slung her so hard against the wall that she bounced off it and back into his stifling embrace.

His right hand squeezed her breast again. The pawing touch of his fingers was like an electric jolt, shocking her out of her panic, leaving only wrath and loathing for this man. And in her raging anger she arched her back, cracked an elbow into Neville's head, and tried to knee his groin, while with her other boot she stamped down on his big feet.

Neville's grip suddenly lightened, and Jessie found her opening, striking his jaw with the heel of first one hand and then the other. She followed through with a murderous punch that traveled about six inches, right to his groin. Neville doubled over to fall, gagging, but Jessie snapped him erect and hit him twice more with the edge of her hand. One chop sent him crashing into the doorframe; the second sent him sprawling on the floor of his parlor.

Before Neville could recover, Jessie retrieved her pistol and returned to press its muzzle against the lawyer's forehead.

"I ought to make you a eunuch," she said bitterly.

Neville gasped, taut with fear. "An error, a mistake—"

"Yours. A nasty error called rape."

There was a rap at the door. "Sir?" It sounded like the butler. He rattled the knob, knocked again. "Sir?" Then there was silence.

Jessie counted off a minute, then drew her pistol back, leaving a livid pink mark on his brow. "I don't hold grudges, though," she said, rising. "Cough up the key. While you're at it, take off your coat and boots."

Neville was breathing a little more normally now. But his fingers shook as he first handed Jessie the door key, then rolled to his knees to remove his suit jacket, and finally tottered ungainly on each leg while he tugged off his boots. "There, now—"

"Now your vest and shirt." Oblivious to her uncovered state, she watched Neville glumly unbutton his vest, undo his celluloid collar, and open his white dress shirt to slide it over his head.

"Go on. Galluses and trousers are next."

"Listen here—"

"You'd think," she said wearily, "you were different from other males." Her voice harshened. "You want me to help you?"

"N-no." Neville unhitched his suspenders, tossed them aside, then dropped his trousers and stepped out of them. He was wearing only black socks and garters now, and Egyptian cotton drawers.

Jessica waggled the pistol. "Socks and garters can stay."

"You cannot be serious!"

"Tempt me," she said venomously. "Your equipment is pretty standard, and you sure wanted to wave it my way a few minutes ago. Now get in tune with nature, or I'll shoot your damn drawers off."

Fumbling, Neville stripped off his underwear and stood, virtually naked, before Jessica's mocking appraisal. "For a big man, you're kind of small," she said contemptuously.

Neville scowled. "You've had your fun. Now get out."

"Not in this blouse." Jessie scooped up Neville's dress shirt and backed a short distance away so she could keep him at bay while she changed. She peeled to her waist, her nude torso ivoried by the lamplight, then donned his shirt and her denim jacket. The tattered shreds of her blouse she left on the floor as she moved to unlock the door. She touched her jacket pocket to make sure the map was still in it, then gave Neville a wintery smile.

He responded with a frigid glare of hatred.

Without a word, Jessie stepped out and locked the door from the hall side. She hurried along the hallway to the front door, her coppery hair straggling in disorder down her back, the shirt tight across her bosom and bunching out where she'd hastily tucked it in at her waist. But there was defiance in her green eyes, and she held her head high as she hastened out into the smoky air of Virginia City, which seemed fresh in comparison to the atmosphere of Neville's parlor.

★

Chapter 10

By the time Jessie descended the hill to C Street, she had walked off the heat of her fury. She turned onto the busy crosstown street, feeling her rage congeal to cold indignation, then freeze slowly into an abiding resentment that would, she vowed, earn Mr. Neville a chilly reception should they ever chance to meet again.

In her preoccupation, she almost missed seeing Gabe Winthrop heading toward her. He was driving Mastleg Thistle's doddery wagon, and almost missed seeing Jessie as he concentrated on guiding the cranky mule through the traffic. When they did catch sight of each other, Jessie waved, and Gabe swung in past the horse-lined hitch rail of a noisy saloon, halting in a space along the boardwalk.

"Can I give you a lift?" he called.

Jessie saved her response until she was close enough to be heard over the noise from the adjacent saloon. By then she'd spotted the supplies in the wagon and

Gabe's horse tied to the tailgate, and guessed he was leaving for his claim. She shook her head. "Thanks, but my hotel's the wrong way for you, and there's no need to put you to the trouble."

"Can't put me to more trouble than I got already," he growled meanly. Then, as if to cover his anger, he said hastily, "No trouble, Jessie. Was makin' a night of travelin' anyhow, stoppin' at Mastleg's to park his wagon and tend his animals. I'm in no hurry to get home."

She wondered why Gabe referred to the property as Mastleg's instead of Unity's, whose property it all was now. Thinking better of correcting him, she took out the map Neville had drawn and handed it up. "Ki and I will be out near you tomorrow. Can you point out your camp on this?"

Gabe turned the map to get the sense of it, and was frowning studiously at it when the saloon's batwings flapped open and a drunk staggered out. The man ogled them and approached in a weaving path. "Shay, buddy," he said, "you found yourself a sweetie, didn'tcha?"

"Go sleep it off, mister," Gabe replied.

"Don't ice up on me," the drunk said, and belched. "You ain't the only feller who's got a honey-hole." He winked at Jessie with a leer, leaning forward almost to the point of toppling as he produced a pint from his hip pocket and offered her a drink.

Jessie said, "No," and her face showed a tinge of color when Gabe put the map aside and stepped down. The drunk pressed the bottle on him then, but Gabe fended off the hand and pushed him back from the wagon.

"Don't get tough with me, buddy," the drunk said, losing his friendliness. He leaned his slack weight against Gabe's stiffened arm and tried to take a step forward, but his spur caught on a loose plank. Withdrawing his arm suddenly, Gabe lashed out, and the

106

drunk fell into the punch. Gabe turned away, letting the drunk sag. The spur, still caught, made a soft tinkle as the shank snapped.

Without a word, Gabe put a hand on Jessie's arm, boosted her up into the wagon, and mounted alongside her. He snapped the reins and the mule obeyed for once, moving out into the street. When he could, he turned the wagon around and headed in the direction of her hotel.

There was a flush to Gabe's face that betrayed his feelings. When he shifted to speak to her, Jessie also saw that one of his reddened cheeks had an odd pink blotch, like the imprint of a hand. Whatever had caused it had been recent, and it would soon fade away, but apparently self-conscious of it now, Gabe rubbed it as he spoke.

"I can show you my camp on your li'l map, Jessie. Be glad to. But if that X on it is where you're riding tomorrow, you sure will follow a long swing to get there, and it strikes me you an' Ki would be better off comin' with me, takin' the short leg over from Mastleg's."

"I'd like to save time," Jessie said, tempted yet dubious, "but we'd have to rent horses now, and where would we sleep tonight?"

"At my digs. Or Pa's house—he's better equipped for visitors. And Mastleg's got a couple of geldings better'n skinflint Flynn's crowbait, just standing in his lean-to, in sore need of an airing."

"Well, let's see what Ki is doing. We've rooms at the Palace."

"One Palace, comin' up . . ."

When they reached the hotel, Jessie found that Ki had not yet returned. She took the opportunity to change out of Neville's dress shirt, choosing a snug woolen shirt that would be warm in the crisp mountain air. Then, in a quick note on the back of the map, she

107

instructed Ki to meet her in the morning at Noah Winthrop's ranch. Leaving the note, she went out to where Gabe was patiently waiting.

"Ki isn't around. Is your offer open for one?"

Gabe nodded, straight-faced, and said, "Now stop twisting my arm."

They set out, leaving Virginia City on the same southern route. The flare of campfires speckled the slopes, flickering against the night, the crimson reflections of those lining the trail dancing now and then on the scuffed wooden sides of the wagon. For a number of miles, Jessie and Gabe made no attempt to converse, then Gabe took out a cheap two-for-a-nickel cigar and bit off its end, and that prompted Jessica to break the silence.

"It takes a special man to handle a drunk like you did."

Puzzled, he looked at her. "Don't see nothing special about it a-tall. I just was in no mood to let him have his way with you."

"Not many men can recognize the right thing to do, and do it with every instinct rebelling against it. You wanted to do more than stop him; you wanted to hurt him—hurt him badly—didn't you?"

"I wanted to tear him apart," he admitted savagely.

"But you held back. Because it would've caused a scene and embarrassed me. Thank you for that, Gabe." She smiled and touched his arm lightly. "Do you always do the right thing, even when you hate to?"

"Y'know, you should see the pretty flowers here in the spring."

"All right, so I'm a nosy woman after all. I'm sorry."

"Don't apologize to me." He leaned closer, covering her hand with his. "I didn't get mad at that fellow. I was already mad, and he only made me madder, and I wanted to take it all out on him. On a man, y' see, 'cause a man ain't allowed to beat up a

108

woman." His voice grew increasingly bitter. "Even if the woman is a hellcat, nothing but promising smiles and come-hither eyes!"

Jessie sighed. "Kind of gone on Unity, aren't you?"

Gabe struck a match and lit his cigar. "Yeah, well, you'll hear it from her anyway. I asked her to marry me and make something of the Monteplata together. Damn her! Damn women!" He flung the match away and sank into a moody, private silence, puffing his cigar.

Jessie suspected this wasn't the first time Unity had refused Gabe. Evidently she liked him too much to quit leading him on, yet she was too proud and independent to let him "save" her from the Silverado, and was too distrustful to risk any faith and belief in a loving marriage. But the problem was theirs to solve, Jessie knew, and she refrained from advising or consoling.

Instead, she respected Gabe's unspoken brooding for the rest of the journey to Mastleg's. As the campfires grew fewer, she watched the darkness deepen, admiring the diamond spray of stars, and enjoying the glow of the moon as it fought a losing battle with the shadows of trees and crags. But it was sufficiently brilliant to bathe the clearing around Mastleg's cabin, so that when they finally arrived, they didn't need to light a fire or any lanterns.

The mule was unhitched and fed by the stream, along with a few chickens and two roans—both geldings, as Gabe had claimed, but so grizzle-coated and knock-kneed that he had to admit they were inherited from Enoch Balsam. Jessie picked the less swaybacked of the pair, and while she rummaged through some worn gear, Gabe hobbled the other horse and the mule so they could forage without wandering too far afield.

From his supplies, which he transferred from the wagon to his saddlebags, Gabe brought fresh biscuits and beef strips. A scrubbed-out fruit can served in lieu of Mastleg's tar-caked, rancid-smelling coffee-pot.

Jessie enjoyed their break, despite her uneasiness at the tension Gabe's surliness was causing. For his part, Gabe knew he was lousy company, and felt all the worse about it because he genuinely liked Jessie, who he knew by now wasn't like other rich, influential women he'd met, who wore gaudy clothes and put on snooty airs. With her warmth and genuine charm, Jessie had a natural grace that put the snobs to shame—and put him to shame as well, in his present mood. He felt like a prime, brassbound fool.

They were mounting their horses to pull out when Gabe apologized. "Sorry, Jessie, I acted stupid, and I oughta know better. Strange how a grown man will let one little thing hex him all over."

"There are many strange things," she said gently, wanting to get off the subject. "The Monteplata, for instance. It seems worthless, but it must have some value to somebody, to have cost so many lives."

"Maybe so, but nobody's tagged that train loot, and I'll bet against any rich strikes yet to be found." Gabe clucked his horse into motion, and added, "There's lots of interests in Virginia City, some of 'em pullin' and tuggin' for no earthly reason 'cept the sheer love of fightin'. Maybe that's it."

They swung past the cabin, heading out on the trail that Gabe's father and brothers had used that morning. It soon funneled down to a meager path that began lifting toward somber crests, corkscrewing as it rose to a cleft in the saddleback ridge, then tapered into a pass between moon-blotting palisades of striated rock.

Slow and close they rode, unable to talk much but polite and attentive when they could, increasingly aware of each other. A rapport was forming—and more, as Jessie began to sense that Gabe was growing intrigued with her, and found herself responding to his interest with her own rising interest in him...

110

From the pass, the path dipped into jagged, rubbled terrain where only renegades and predators would care to tread. When the air suddenly chilled and quivered with a dew-laden roar, Jessie realized they were approaching a cataract of some sort. Shortly she could view a gorge threading along diagonally to the path, slab-sided and ax-blade narrow, the Dishwater Creek surging rampant along a series of rapids. The gorge wound on its way, and the path spiraled to a slender bench, then descended, twisting among timber and stone, to a small notch in the floor of a valley.

Once clear of the notch, Jessie folded her hands on her saddlehorn and surveyed the open valley. It was hard-packed and gravelly, too upland to be lush, yet it was tufted with hardy grass and dotted with thickets, and she could glimpse some white clumps of bedded sheep.

"This doesn't look like half-bad range for sheep," she observed.

"Well, it ain't fit for cattle," Gabe allowed. "But having year-round water and the hills to box 'em in, Pa swears he can graze a thousand woolies here without no herders." He gestured to his right. "Pa's got the space. His ranch is a good couple hours of riding yet."

Turning westward, they loped along side by side, flanking the northern cliffs they'd just crossed. Jessie could barely see across to where the parallel southern wall slanted upward, and the valley behind and ahead of her was lost in murky distance.

The footing grew softer as they skirted a shallow depression that was collecting underground seepage from the creek. Suddenly Gabe reined in tightly and leaned over to peer closely at the moist earth.

"What is it?"

"Some real fresh sign, of sheep herdin' t'other way," he answered grimly. "Sheep ain't cattle. Sheep hate to get their hooves wet and seldom step into

111

water, meanin' they was shoved through here."
Straightening, he pulled his carbine from its saddle
boot and slewed his horse around. "Excuse me, Jessie,
while I go do a little chore. Honest herders don't roust
even a small band like this off their bed ground at
night."

Jessie didn't say a word, but swiftly reversed direction and joined Gabe as he headed down the long
eastward stretch of valley.

Gabe scowled at her and the pistol in her fist. "You
should've stayed back, gal. Now save us both some
fretting, and don't try to get close enough to hit anything with your popgun."

In reply, Jessie stuck her tongue out at him.

When the pair had galloped their horses for nearly
a mile, they caught the faint tinkle of a bell somewhere
ahead. They slowed to a trot, searching, but hearing
nothing more. Then, abruptly, they perceived the hazy
silhouettes of sheep and riders.

Again they quickened their pace, hoping to gain a
better look at the horsemen. The shadowy figures
began to take shape, five of them, features masked
by broad-brimmed hats pulled low, as they trail-herded
a small massed flock of ewes and bucks.

"Appears we've snared a—" The splintering crack
of a rifle cut short Gabe's words, and he ducked as
a bullet whined by his head.

The flash of the shot came from some brush not
more than two hundred yards ahead, undoubtedly from
the rear guard for the others who were drifting the
sheep some distance beyond. Jessie wrenched the
gelding toward the scrub; but Gabe stood up in his
stirrups and triggered his carbine. Close on the heels
of his shot came the sound of brush crashing and a
man's sharp cry of pain. A riderless horse vaulted out
of the scrub and raced away.

By now the others were pulling their horses about,
shouldering rifles and bringing them into play. Gabe

shouted, "Stay put!" and drove straight at the raiders. Jessie, aware that his reckless charge was prompted by fears for her safety, spurred after him, not about to rest on the sidelines while he drew all the fire.

Together they shot several times in rapid order, but their targets were elusive, swaying and lurching as plaintively bleating sheep milled around and under their horses. The raiders' aim was thrown off even worse and, stymied, they began pulling free of the panicky sheep and hunting for shelter. But there was no shelter; brush patches were few and far between, and too scrawny to provide much cover.

Bullets were traded at a furious rate, searing the air and kicking up grit, whining off boulders and an occasional tree. Jessie swerved her horse to attack at a tangent and avoid the panicky sheep. Gabe bagged one of the five raiders then, the rider folding from his saddle as his horse spooked. Jessie was in close enough now, and winged a second man in his upper right chest; he clutched at his reins, straining to catch up with the remaining three, who had already turned to flee eastward.

Gabe and Jessie rode after them. The wounded man slumped over, and lost his seat when his horse shied from a grazing bullet. The others, twisting about, opened up with a prolonged rain of lead to cover their retreat.

Jessie saw the flame-lancing discharges, and heard the slugs whistling about her. She goaded her horse on, her own weapon bucking in her hand. Suddenly a bright flaring light seemed to jar her eyes, and she grabbed sickly for her saddlehorn, her entire upper body insensible. She'd been shot; instinctively she knew she'd been struck by a bullet high in her left lung or shoulder, though she was so numb from the shock that she couldn't locate the center of her injury.

Unable to draw a breath, her ears ringing, her vision gradually dimming, Jessie clung wavering to the horn, subconsciously aware that the horse had veered and stopped. She had a vague sense of falling, falling, never hurriedly, never harmfully.

Then there was another blinding flash within her head, and the steady downward motion eased into black oblivion.

★

Chapter 11

"Jessie!"

Gabe, having kept an anxious eye on her throughout the fray, stared horrified when she stiffened from
sudden impact, and then slipped from her saddle.
Frantically he wheeled about, his horse stumbling and
rearing, while beyond, the three surviving sheep raiders were still cursing and shooting as they bolted for
the far end of the valley.

Launching himself across the open stretch, Gabe
sent another swift volley at them. He shouted Jessie's
name several times, but got no response. He feared
she was either dead or too badly wounded to move
or call out. The firing dwindled as the men increased
their distance, abandoning their downed companions
and their stolen, scattered flock. The last echoes of
gunfire had faded away when Gabe hauled his horse
to a stop, and dove to the ground in a sliding run.

"Say somethin', Jessie! Please!" Kneeling, he
peered at her unmoving features, which looked as

waxen and pale as the moonlight striking them. He dropped his head to her chest, and after a moment he sighed tremulously, having picked up a faint yet regular pulse.

"Thank God." He glanced around for signs of the raiders sneaking back, then spread open her jacket and tipped her from side to side, probing for obvious wounds as gently as he could.

"Might still be busted up fierce inside," he murmured, checking again for any returning men. "Can't stay here. Have to risk it."

Lifting Jessie in his arms, Gabe tenderly maneuvered her over her saddle. He scooped up her fallen pistol, gathered the reins of both horses, and then, with his carbine hooked under his arm, Gabe began a slow, cautious walk to the base of the nearest cliff— which was still a fair trek across the valley floor.

Eventually he reached a small wedge of aspens, in behind a low screen of heather and rocks. Stripping his horse, he laid out its saddle blanket on the rough ground, then eased Jessie's slack body down and, uncorking his canvas water bag, cradled her head in his lap while he tried to force a few drops between her lips.

Choking, moaning, Jessie swallowed.

"Atta girl," Gabe soothed. "Drink up."

"Wha—what happened?"

He grinned. "When you get steadier, you tell me."

She stirred feebly, sipping again, remaining quiet until she recovered sufficiently to allow herself to be propped up. "Not . . . very clear. I seem to recall being hit, an awful shock, dropping . . ."

"Sure 'nough, you've got a bump on your noggin big's a goose egg, but there ain't no blood or holes on you that I could see."

"Well, I didn't fall asleep off my saddle," she said, and began struggling to remove her jacket. "Help me."

"Now look—I mean, that is—"

116

"Gabe, I won't die of modesty, but I can from a gunshot wound."

His face burning, he gingerly slipped off her jacket, then hesitantly unbuttoned the snug, woolen shirt she was wearing, and peeled it back away from her shoulder. His embarrassment vanished and was replaced by puzzlement when he saw a large bruise high on her left breast, with a small cut at its center. He sat back on his heels and scratched his head.

"Danged if I can figure this," he said, and probed delicately with his fingers around the area of the bruise. Jessie winced, but only looked at him quizzically. Obviously his probing wasn't causing her as much pain as a bullet wound should.

"What is it?" she asked.

"Well," he said, untying the bandanna around his neck, "you ask me, it don't even look like the slug went in. Don't look like a proper bullet wound a-tall." He poured some water on the bandanna and daubed at the cut. It had already begun to clot over. His hand trembled a bit, and the pulse at the base of his throat picked up a rapid, irregular beat. And Jessie, aware of his consternation, sensed a perverse reaction budding in her.

"I'll help you dress now," he suggested.

"In a while, thanks. I think I'll let it dry first, and the air should be good for healing. That is, unless it bothers you?"

"Not if it don't bother you," he said, but his voice was shaky. Her composure astonished him, increasing his admiration. Death didn't often come so close to a woman as it had to her, yet Jessie was leaning back on her elbows with healthy color returning to her cheeks, her eyes vibrant, her breathing calmer than his own. Fumbling, he took her pistol out of his belt and placed it by her on the blanket.

"I'm going for a fast gander," he explained, standing up. He tousled her hair and leaned to assure her

117

with a brotherly peck, but Jessie shifted unexpectedly, and their lips brushed in a teasing kiss, his hand accidentally touching her breast. The light, sliding contact sent intriguing tingles radiating through Jessie's flesh, and Gabe straightened, electrified and embarrassed, almost stammering. "Y-yeah, try an' rest, but be ready to start firing. No reason to trust anyone, not even me."

"Not even you?"

"Trust no man, and you won't never get catched off guard." Gabe tried to say it solemnly, but his voice faltered at the end, and he found it difficult to look at her as he mounted her gelding and rode away.

Jessie stretched wearily, still feeling weak and woozy, her head hurting at intervals. But taking a nap proved impossible, and even her resting was fitful, her thoughts dwelling on Gabe's flustered behavior. Refreshing, she mused; he'd obviously been aroused, yet unlike Chester Neville, he'd not tried to seduce her. Nor had she tried to provoke him, although she relished the sensation of exciting those few men she found desirable. Desirable? Lord, merely contemplating him was causing an involuntary throb in her loins, and a reflexive hardening of her nipples. No wonder she couldn't rest!

She was anything but weary by the time she heard Gabe return. Dismounting outside the screen, he softly led the gelding to the aspen, secured it near his horse, and began to ease off its gear.

"I'm awake, Gabe."

"Well, I didn't want to disturb you." While he scouted for kindling, he said, "The sheep have bedded again, and them two fellers are cold meat, so they won't need no watching." He came over and dropped a few sticks on the ground. "No hint o' the others. Less'n their horses sprouted wings, it beats me how they got outta the east hills."

Then, squatting, Gabe struck a match and started a tiny fire. He was silent for so long that Jessie im-

118

patiently asked, "Okay, and what's next?"

"Next is what's next," he answered, and settled close beside her. "I ain't no seventh son of a seventh son, able to see the future. I can call your attention to one ringtailed fact, though, which is that yes, ma'am, you were shot." He drew a flattened piece of metal from his shirt pocket and held it up. "This's the slug."

Jessie reached for the bit of lead, her breasts swaying inadvertently against his arm. She carefully paid no attention.

But Gabe certainly noticed. He cleared his throat and said, "I, ah, saw your saddletree was gouged, and a chunk clipped outta the rim of the horn. So I nosed around till I found that bullet." He commenced to stroke the side of her leg idly, with little thought other than that it was pretty. "Way I reckon, the shot struck the tree, mashed, ripped up past the horn, and struck you flat side on."

"I believe you've figured it right, Gabe. I had the wind knocked out of me, and was stunned when I fell." Fascinated, she watched his hand trail back and forth reverently over the contour of her leg, then tilted her face to smile at him. "I'm obliged to you, you know."

They were so close now that Gabe could feel her taut nipples pressing against his shirt. He gazed into her smoldering eyes, finding he was moving his head toward her lips. He stopped.

Her lips, partly open, assumed a taunting expression. "Why don't you kiss me, Gabe? I won't bite, at least not yet."

His arms went around her and he kissed her slowly, savoring the anticipation, remembering to be gentle. A breath later he forgot all his good intentions as fast as she did.

When Jessie finally eased from their soulful kiss, the warmth of her face was like the glow of the fire. Again Gabe paused apprehensively, and she looked deep in his eyes. "No, Gabe. I don't love you." She spoke with fondness. "You're quite a man, you know. Different. I guess that's why I like you. Can't a gal just *like* a fellow?"

He nodded tensely. Yet he still didn't move, as though he was still afraid to lose himself and force his brutality on her. Jessie was lovely, gazing at him so temptingly, so adoringly...

She laughed shyly and unbuckled her belt. Her hands crept within the waistband of her jeans and he heard the pop of the fly's buttons as she squirmed, using both hands. "Well? Help me."

Gabe hesitated only a second this time. With more dexterity than he'd displayed with her blouse, he relieved her of boots and pants, his eyes still on hers and only darting briefly to check the movements of his hands. When she was totally naked, he stared at her curvaceous body as she lay back and beckoned languidly.

"You are...too lovely! May I kiss you, Jessie?"

"Don't ask," she murmured. "Just do."

Kneeling between her feet, Gabe leaned forward to gently taste each breast, then her navel, and then her pubic mound, with lips feverish with desire. He heard her sigh blissfully as he parted her willing legs yet more and slowly laid the fingers of both hands upon her rosy nook. Gradually he pressed the borders slightly apart.

Jessie shuddered. "What sweet torture."

"A rosebud," Gabe whispered, and his mouth fell wetly against it, his tongue snaking out to lick the length of her sensitive crevice.

From the first moment of his wet nibbling impact, Jessie's breathing was a series of convulsive gasps. She could have spent, she felt, at any instant, and she ground her buttocks against the blanket in an effort to restrain herself for a while, and to experience more of the ineffable sensations of Gabe's lascivious mouth.

Gabe seemed to know instinctively how to keep her keyed up to the very verge of orgasm without quite triggering her ultimate release. Her head was thrown back, her ecstatic face turned heavenward, and her spine arched. She heard Gabe pant, though it was partly muffled by her squeezing inner thighs, and then, abruptly, she heard a different-sounding groan. Looking down her quivering nudity, she saw that somehow, without ungluing his mouth from between her legs, Gabe had skillfully managed to undress himself.

Reaching out, her hands caressed his bobbing head, her fingers curling greedily in his hair. "Enough, I want more," she pleaded insensibly. "I . . . I want you in me before I . . . explode!"

Instead, Gabe burrowed deeper in a prolonged, forceful kiss, whipping his mouth up and down until her hips trembled with incandescent fury. She felt herself erupting, her climax just beginning, when Gabe raised his head and lunged up over her, showing a wiry and suntanned body with a very respectable and vastly aroused virility.

Like lightning, her hand dipped to guide his thick erection into her. "Yessss," she sighed, feeling her wet loins parting and hard male flesh driving far up inside her.

Gabe plunged deep into her, his buttocks tightening as he thrust his entire length in a savage passion that rocked them both convulsively. Her hot, tight envelope clung tenaciously to him, sending constant rippling sensations through her.

Grinning in lustful delight, Gabe pumped steadily, swiftly. Jessie quivered at the feel of her inner flesh stretching tightly, and spread her legs wider in an attempt to relieve the strain. Then she bent her knees back almost to her chest to allow Gabe more room, still shivering as she continued to feel herself crammed and filled by his hard shaft. It seemed to hammer into her violently, creating a whirling maelstrom of intense passion and need.

When he lifted himself on his hands and glanced down at their joined flesh, he could see the lacy fringe

121

of her pubic fleece failing to cover all of her gripping pink lips. He could see how her splayed loins clasped his thick barrel in a viselike embrace.

Crushing himself back onto Jessie, Gabe bruised his mouth on hers. Deliriously she accepted his tongue, undulating her hips against his pounding groin, her motions skewering her utterly on his plunging manhood. And all the while Gabe moved rhythmically in the fork of her thighs, spearing in and out of her clenching belly.

Jessie screamed, and climaxed. It left her weak, and she was a limp packet into which Gabe continued to lance. He suddenly cried out, stiffening as he flooded her with his climactic release. He sagged against her, then, drained.

They cuddled close together, drifting in a placid infinity as they dozed dreamlessly. Well, almost. There were three or four times during the night when pleasing interruptions broke into their sleep.

★

Chapter 12

Hours earlier, while Jessie had been meticulously composing her coded telegram to the Circle Star, and Chester Neville had been hastily sending her a note, Ki had circulated through the packed Silverado Club, unaware that the crafty lawyer was already hurrying to the Palace Hotel. All he knew was that somehow, during that short delay caused by Gabe's and Unity's tiff, Neville had managed to disappear.

Annoyed, Ki started rechecking the saloon on the off-chance he'd overlooked Neville in a bathroom or some rear cranny. The tiny stage was empty, Unity's trio not having appeared from the back yet. At a nearby table he glimpsed Francine MacNear, entertaining two roughneck miners who were antagonistically vying for her favors. But no Neville. Neville had gone, though not out the front entrance, Ki was sure, which meant he must have left by a rear exit, which in turn meant he must be buddies with the saloon owner, Grantree, who was leaning at the end of the bar with that possum-faced gunman, engaged in a low-voiced but plainly intense conversation.

Ki maneuvered closer, hoping to catch any stray words. He could now see that Grantree was drinking coffee, while the gunman was swigging whiskey, occasionally fingering a strip of court plaster stuck to his slack jaw. The man had changed clothes since yesterday evening, but not since he'd tried to help hang Gabe; recognizing the shirt, Ki realized that the man's knobby thinness matched the lanky build of the hooded lyncher. He also realized why the man hadn't been wearing a revolver then; riding with his high-jutting Remington, now back in its peculiar quick-draw rig, would have been very uncomfortable, not to mention dangerous if the pistol should accidentally discharge.

The man was standing at an angle, able to view the room behind him in the backbar mirror as he talked to Grantree. Blurting a startled curse, he pivoted to stare at Ki. And Ki, approaching, read Grantree's lips in addition to hearing his quick warning: "Not in here, Lloyd."

"Fancy bumping into you again," Ki said cheerfully to the gunman. "It's positively a wonder how you do get around."

The man frowned. "Get lost, stranger."

Ki beamed. "I always did like hide-and-seek."

"By Gawd, if you was heeled—" Glowering, the gunman named Lloyd stroked the butt of his revolver. "Any more sass, and dammit, unarmed or not, I'll go borrow you a shooter and—"

"Dolores, crack a fresh bottle and anchor it here," Grantree interrupted in a loud order, and clapped friendly hands on the two men's shoulders. "Drinks are on me, gents. Help yourselves while I take my regular tour of the premises." He paused as the half-naked barmaid set a bottle and glasses down, then he poured them a round and, chuckling heartily, moved away from the bar.

Ki lifted his glass. "May snakes poison one another."

"What?" Lloyd almost sloshed his raised drink. "Oh yeah, okay." He gulped the whiskey and quickly refilled their glasses, his eyes growing slyer. "You heard the boss, pal. Have plenty."

Besides feeding each other booze, they didn't palaver much, having nothing in common except mutual antipathy. But Ki figured he'd stay awhile. He'd already lost Neville, and could yet lose his own life, but by brazenly cutting in on Grantree and Lloyd, he'd struck a lead to some of the "coincidences" involving the Silverado. And along with the risks was the chance Grantree might let something slip, or goad Lloyd into making a stupid blunder.

Ki listened to the noises around him—the clink of glasses and the shuffle of feet, the harsh voices foolish with liquor. Unity's bare-breasted cowgirl band came onstage to whistles and stomps. The floor started to shake from the stamping feet of cavorting couples, and Ki glimpsed Francine sharing dances with one miner and then another. A fistfight broke out in a corner, but was speedily squelched by the bouncers, a pair of hulking thugs who took no guff, and promptly armlocked the blustering opponents and hustled them out the front door.

Ki watched the bouncers' efficient teamwork with speculative interest, and failed to notice Francine approaching. "Well," she said, squeezing in beside him. "I hoped I'd see you come back in."

Ki smiled. "Here I am."

Her lower lip was pouty. "Why haven't you rescued me?"

Ki glanced at the miners. They were eyeing Francine and him, and looking irritated about it, too. "Maybe later," he replied, his smile widening. "Don't dance too much. It shortens your sex life."

"I don't care." Frowning, she turned and headed for the miners.

Lloyd snickered and pressed more whiskey on Ki. Although he had a strong head and could outlast most

125

contestants in a drinking bout, Ki began to feign intoxication, because that seemed to be Lloyd's aim. More and more customers entered the saloon, while the three semi-nude musicians played for the throng. The Silverado roared with happy if crude exhilaration.

Slurring his voice in pretended tipsiness, Ki said, "I wanna request a tune I learned on my ma's knee."

"You're stickin' here. Anyhow, you can't go ask—"

"Gotta be movin', Lloyd. See you tomorrow, p'raps." Ki walked unsteadily across the dance floor. Francine danced by, studiously ignoring him while concentrating on the miner who was holding her. Ki paid no attention to her ploy, but sneaked a glance behind him, and saw that not only was Lloyd provoked into coming after him, but Grantree was glaring his way, hands bunched on hips, from beside the office door.

Ki continued wandering toward the stage. Reaching its steps, he grinned up at Unity, reading the pain in her face and wondering how she could entertain with the sorrow in her heart. She never missed a note, but gave him a look as if exasperated by his apparent drunkenness.

He called, "Can we meet later?"

"If you're sober," she retorted over the music.

Lloyd arrived, and flashed a false smile. "Let's go, pal."

"I like it right here, Lloyd."

"Ki, please go. I have to work." Unity nodded toward Grantree, who was now motioning to her, signaling her to stop fraternizing and tend to fiddling. And Ki, just to prod Lloyd, scoffed, "He can't buy all of you, for the price of your fiddle."

"He thinks so." Unity stepped back, turning aside.

Lloyd's snakelike eyes were glittering wickedly. "Cuss your smartass mouth!" he snarled, spinning Ki to face him. His ill-concealed hostility rose to Ki's snare, hooking on this good, vaguely chivalrous ex-

126

cuse. "You son of a bitch, you, I'll teach you manners!"

His left fist shot out for Ki's face, but even as it sped through the air, Ki's swifter fingers caught Lloyd's wrist in a grasp like a steel claw, checking the punch with ridiculous ease.

"Make it soft on yourself, Lloyd, and don't start anything in front of this nice lady. Go suck up your rotgut and forget it."

There was cool amusement in Ki's quiet voice, and it stoked Lloyd's anger to fiery rage. Self-control snapping, he swore and went for his revolver, but before he could clear leather, those same steely fingers closed on his right wrist. This time Ki accentuated his lesson. Lloyd's swearing turned to a bark of agony as Ki's grip ground his wristbones together, forcing his hand to open spasmodically and release his revolver. Infuriated beyond sense, Lloyd instantly swung his left again in a crushing uppercut. Once more his fist missed his mark. He was whirled about, his arm bent cruelly behind his back, and the intolerable leverage on his elbow and shoulder brought him up on his boot toes, his face convulsing with pain.

"What in Hades!" Grantree and his bouncers pushed their way through the boisterous, incurious mob. "Let Lloyd go," Grantree ordered without much malice. "I won't stand for trouble. From anybody."

Ki appraised the two bouncers. The closer of the two was a hardcase with a slouching stance, and the other was a shorter but stockier brute with a droopy mustache. Both were eager for blood. Still he hesitated, though in truth the game was over, and this was the time to end it.

Shrugging, he released Lloyd, who lurched forward a pace before twisting around, teeth bared and spite burning in his eyes.

"Fine," Grantree said, nodding. "Now go get some air."

Ki rubbed an earlobe. The bouncers were still eye-

127

ing him venomously. Lloyd was staring at him, but the hand hovering by his revolver was a greater menace. From onstage, Unity was observing him intently. Ki hadn't counted on this, but it fit into his improvised plans, and to argue could only get people hurt, including Unity and himself.

"Not a bad idea. Think I will take a breather." Ki grinned amiably and started for the door.

Grantree remained, watching him leave. So did Lloyd, his mouth now clamped shut like a beartrap, as the man who'd held him ranting and helpless moved in an erratic weaving course for the entrance.

Ki's stagger lasted until he had wound along the boardwalk past the pirate doorman's range of vision. Then he dipped into an alley between two buildings, flattened himself against a wall, and waited.

A moment later Ki spotted Lloyd hurrying toward him, his hand dangling near his revolver. Ki was pleased to see that he'd gobbled the bait and was now trailing the lure away from the Silverado. Out here, Lloyd would quickly learn that the new game wouldn't be easy foolery, like the first one. Ki was ready to teach him, prepared to give Lloyd a fairer chance than Lloyd proposed to give him. And if Lloyd ended his lessons by lying horizontal, unable to lynch miners or waylay drunks, Ki was grimly ready to oblige him.

He poised in the obscuring shadows, hearing Lloyd approach the alley, when suddenly Grantree's voice shouted, "Lloyd! C'mere!"

Lloyd came up short with a startled breath. Grantree called, "I wish to talk to you. Now." There was a scuffled hesitation, then Ki could hear Lloyd's bootsteps and curses receding toward the saloon.

Immediately Ki turned and hastened down the alleyway to the rear of the buildings. He sprinted along the hilly, trash-heaped backyards, finding, as he ran the impromptu obstacle course, that all the whiskey he'd consumed was slightly affecting his coordination. But his brain was sober, and was working furiously.

Reaching the corner of the building across from the Silverado, he drew in and listened, scanning the area. About a quarter of the way up the alley, Ki saw that the Silverado had a recessed side door, with a tiny stoop and a tinier overhang. There were no other doors, and the few windows were boarded over, and when Ki darted fleetingly to check the saloon's rear, he found that its windows and one door were also planked over.

Moving to the side door, Ki wondered if Grantree's crude barricades were to keep his working girls in or nonpaying gents out. Probably both, he decided, putting an ear to the door. Hearing nothing, he took a thin, pliant strip of metal from inside his vest, then hunkered down on the stoop and picked the door lock.

Warily he snicked the latch back and pushed the door. Satisfied, he eased inside, closing the door behind him. As his eyes adjusted to the darkness, he found that he was standing in a large pantry. Directly ahead was a double-doored entry to a kitchen. The kitchen was unoccupied, but its clutter of foodstuffs and utensils showed that it was in constant use. On Ki's right, a long corridor extended to a closed door. Up on the wall beside the door was a bracket lamp, its low flame supplying the corridor's only illumination.

He gently slid shut the double doors and padded noiselessly up the dimly lit corridor. He made it even dimmer, reaching out and turning even lower the wick of the bracket lamp, then flattening himself against the closed door. He caught the muffled uproar and music from the saloon area—but he'd even heard that noise while still outside.

This door was unlocked. Gradually Ki cracked the door ajar until it was wide enough for him to slip through, into a windowless room smelling of liquor

129

and cigar smoke. By the bright glow of a parlor lamp suspended from the ceiling, Ki saw that what he'd sneaked into was the office; through an archway was an adjacent room, also lamplit, which appeared to be Grantree's living quarters. Jackpot!

The door to the saloon was lacking its key and didn't have a separate deadbolt, so Ki stayed sharply alert for a turning knob or approaching steps, as he undertook a swift ransacking of the office.

Centered in the office was a massive flat desk of battered mahogany, resting with a mismatched swivel chair on a soiled Oriental carpet. Facing the desk were three hardbacked chairs, and a squat safe that Ki ignored as soon as he discovered it was locked. Behind the desk was a wall of filing cabinets and bookshelves, which, like the desktop and drawers, were crammed with papers.

Ki foraged through the litter, rifling the desk, files, and shelves; searching through binders and odd stacks of ledgers; examining documents, accounts, and records. He even rummaged in the wastebasket. He missed little but found little, other than some decks of shaved playing cards and sets of loaded dice.

Next he combed the adjacent room. Besides the brass bed, there was a carved oak dresser and wardrobe set, and a commode fashioned like a chair, with a lid over its seat. The usual washbasin and pitcher stood on the dresser, along with a man's leather toilet outfit, and in the dresser were shirts and socks and flannel underwear. A few suits hung in the wardrobe, with discarded clothing shoved in a corner.

The jackpot, Ki concluded disgustedly, was a bust.

He was leaving the bedroom when he heard talking outside the saloon door, the voices garbled by the door and the general blare. He moved back to the bedroom as someone began fumbling with the doorknob, and slipped inside the wardrobe, among the suits and dumped clothes. While he was easing the wardrobe doors closed, the saloon door opened.

"Shut it," Grantree's unmistakable voice said.

As the door slammed, Ki heard, "Missed him, damn well missed," and recognized the other voice as Lloyd's. "By Gawd, if you hadn't drug me back to help your bouncers, I'd have found him."

There was the squeak of a chair; Ki guessed Grantree was sitting down. "Astounds me, the luck of some drunks, but you'll have other chances. Control, Lloyd, control."

"Control, my bleedin' ass!"

"Then put it this way. We can't afford to have you traipsing all over town on a private vendetta," Grantree said curtly. "We brought you here, and we expect you to stay here until your specific task is done, no more and no less. Lloyd, we're counting on you."

"Only reason you count on me is 'cause I'm the only one who'll handle them fuckers. Well, her accident's all set. It could've happened already, and might during one of her breaks, but no later'n when she hits beddy-bye tonight. Hell, my job's all done."

"Your job's not done till *she's* done," Grantree countered, his chair squeaking as if he were rising. "But I don't want any more trouble, and you fly off the handle too easily, Lloyd. Yes, I think it'd be best if you kept out of the bar area and to the kitchen."

"The hell! I won't—"

"You *will*," Grantree cut in, his tone brooking no argument. "You'll stay here, out of trouble, and in the kitchen. Understand?"

Lloyd didn't answer.

"Understand?" Grantree repeated.

"Yeah."

"Fine. Now I've got to spruce up a bit. You won't find it bad, y'know. There's a ton of food to eat, and a bottle of bonded rye in one of the cupboards." Grantree's voice was becoming louder as he neared the bedroom. "Trust me, Lloyd, it's for your own good."

The saloon door opened to a rowdy blast, and Grantree halted by the archway. "The other door, Lloyd! Take the back hall."

The saloon door closed. "Yeah, sorry."

"And Lloyd, I mean it, trust me." Grantree's voice grew genial again. "Men have taken us for fools, but they're wrong. You string along with us, and you'll get rich helping us prove them all wrong. And you're not dumb, Lloyd. We're counting on you."

"Thanks."

From the slit between the loosely closed wardrobe doors, Ki saw Grantree enter and move hastily toward the commode, while, from the office, he heard Lloyd angle toward the hall door. Ki crouched motionless as Grantree, his back to the wardrobe, one-handedly opened his trouser fly while the other hand lifted the seat lid. The hall door banged. Grantree, head bent to watch his aim, sighed as he began urinating noisily into the commode's hidden chamber pot.

And Ki sprang out of the wardrobe.

He crossed the small room in three hushed steps. Grantree had time for a distracted "Lloyd?" before Ki landed behind him, the callused edges of both hands axing into either side of Grantree's exposed neck.

Grantree's head snapped forward, the crown of his skull cracking the back panel of the commode. The commode tilted, and he tripped on the suddenly exposed chamber pot. The whole works toppled on its side, the commode fracturing, the chamber pot spilling, and Grantree sprawling limply, never stirring but still unconsciously pissing.

Before Grantree hit the floor, Ki was racing out into the office. He glanced at the saloon door, tempted to go out that way. But this wasn't mere escape; he must escape unseen, before Grantree woke from his unintentional wet nap.

He realized that if he was to do that, his odds were better against one person than they were against a whole crowded saloon. Even so, it would be difficult

132

to avoid being spotted by Lloyd if he was already in the kitchen. His only chance was that the man was still in the hallway, walking away from Grantree's quarters. In less time than it took to consider this, Ki was at the hall door.

Snaking the latch open, Ki quietly swung the door just enough to slide by, while swiftly reaching around to palm the other knob. He turned as he squeezed through, so that while clearing the door he was also closing it, one hand behind him controlling the knob, the other stretching high to extinguish the hall bracket lamp.

In that instant, Ki grinned thinly in relief as he spotted Lloyd muttering sourly to himself, sauntering a distance ahead but still some yards from the pantry. Then Ki smothered the lamp, pinching the wick of its faint-burning flame, and the corridor was plunged into a darkness as black as the inside of a cave.

"What the fuck!"

Ki eased forward on cat feet. "Lloyd," he called in a near whisper, risking a poor imitation of Grantree's voice to draw the gunman.

"Silas, is that you? Mr. Grantree?"

Ki thought he could hear Lloyd fumbling his way along the wall. He figured that Remington was already in his hand.

"Hey, Mr. Grantree? Get a lamp, why don'tcha?"

Ki went down the darkened corridor with long, silent strides, unwilling to pull a weapon for the same reason he'd lured Lloyd outside. Mine-country justice could be speedy and harsh on a stranger who killed someone in a local, popular, and seemingly legitimate establishment. And Ki, who sensed that a settling of accounts was coming due soon, didn't wish to give Grantree and his crew any legal excuse to defang him before it fell time to collect the Silverado's debts, with interest.

"At least strike a match! Dammit, Grantree, sing out!"

Moving closer, Ki was reviewing the unarmed tactics he'd use, when he realized he couldn't rely on his martial skills; it would be tantamount to leaving a calling card. He'd have to resort to the common method here, the brawl, and hope that despite its comparative clumsiness and inefficiency, he could end the fight quickly.

"Where the hell are you, Grantree?" There was whiskey, suspicion, and a killer's fury in the rasp of Lloyd's voice. "What kind o' hoodwink are you trying to put over on a man?"

Guided by Lloyd's voice, Ki approached with swift, light steps on the balls of his feet. He now had his arms cocked in a casual boxer's stance, and was clenching and unclenching his hands into fists, when he bumped blindly into Lloyd.

Having expected this might happen, Ki was prepared, and pushed forward. Lloyd, caught by surprise, was shoved further off balance and wavered a step back, giving Ki room to take a short-range poke at his jaw. But in the utter blackness, Ki's fist merely grazed his cheek, then furrowed up across his lips and socked him squarely in the nostrils.

His nose gushed blood. The Remington flamed, Lloyd's pained cursing lost in its blast. Its bullet thrummed past Ki's ear and plowed into the office door far behind, while Ki charged at the muzzle flash, his only way to pinpoint Lloyd in the dark. Before Lloyd could aim his revolver for another shot, Ki barged into him and closed with drumming right-left combinations to body and head, and a jolting series of strikes to stymie his gun hand while lunging after the revolver.

Lloyd shifted and feinted and counterpunched, frantic to evade the insistent fists long enough to swing his revolver into action. He wasn't a pugilist—few gunslicks were—but his body was gristle and rawhide and a glutton for punishment. He absorbed Ki's pistoning of his belly and face, and lashed back defensively, butting Ki hard and knocking him away a pace. In that moment he broke free.

Then Ki caught a sound like Lloyd turning, and taking a step toward the noise, he hammered out a one-two tracer. He felt the jarring contact, his left ripping a gash over Lloyd's right eye, his right squashing the bridge of Lloyd's ruptured nose.

Spraying fresh blood, Lloyd blundered into a corridor wall, triggering reflexively. Ki pursued, hearing Lloyd's squawl of agony again being drowned out by his revolver's report. The shot slewed away wildly and drilled through the ceiling.

Ki ignored it, concentrating on Lloyd, stabbing two swift rights to his heart, Lloyd grunted, shuddering. Ki, hoping this was a sign that the thug was finally weakening, reached out his left hand and grabbed his gun wrist.

Lloyd struggled frenziedly, wrenching and yanking, cursing in a bubbly, clotted voice. Firming his grip, Ki used a corkscrewing right fist to slug Lloyd first in the breastbone, very low, and then in the solar plexus with an upward hook. Lloyd's lungs emptied of air with a loud *whoosh*.

Ki jockeyed his hold on Lloyd's wrist, cracked it across his rising knee, and with his right hand plucked the revolver out of Lloyd's nerveless fingers and tossed it far into the blackness. Then, without hesitation, Ki bored in with a combination to Lloyd's gut, and struck him a half-dozen more times in his nose and eyes.

Lloyd began sagging, reeling from the assault. Ki propelled a right fist to Lloyd's jaw, but Lloyd was now listing at a leftward angle, and Ki's uppercut crunched with meaty impact against Lloyd's left jawline, just below his temple. Lloyd straightened in an arc to the right, then kept on curving over to hit the floor, where he stayed.

Ki groped toward the pantry, feeling his way along the corridor wall. He fumbled open the outside door, crossed the alley, and faded along the rear of the buildings again to the first alley he'd taken. Then he retraced his steps up it to the street.

Nobody had seen him to recognize him. Even bellied up close and facing Lloyd, identification had been impossible in that black abyss. He wondered just how Lloyd and Grantree would iron out their suspicions and arguments. Each of them apparently had reason to fear a double-cross, there being no honor among such thieves.

Ki would have chuckled, if it weren't for the thought of Unity. She was a lone girl surrounded by tough, coldblooded, crooked enemies—for, even without solid evidence, Ki was positive the Silverado was a prime rathole of the Posse Comitatus. Undoubtedly Lloyd was a top henchman, having bossed the lynchers and probably helped to direct the ambush that killed Mastleg. In turn, Lloyd was under Grantree's orders, though there had been references to someone else, an employer or partner who, like Grantree and Lloyd, would stoop to anything—anything at all— including plots to rig "accidental" deaths.

And while Ki hadn't overheard Grantree and Lloyd mention Unity by name, he was convinced that she was the one their murder scheme was planned for. Anytime now, perhaps during one of her breaks, but certainly before the night was over, Lloyd had promised.

Unity didn't know it yet, but she was fighting for more than her pride and livelihood. That girl was fighting for her life.

Chapter 13

Ki wobbled up to the Silverado, bumped the hitch rail, and was ushered inside by the doorman, who was unaware of his earlier eviction.

The stocky bouncer was at the bar, momentarily facing away. Instantly Ki burrowed into the concealing crowd, scanning the swirl and ebb for other problem spots as he thrust straight toward the stage. There was no sign of Francine, to his relief; she might have unwittingly delayed or called attention to him. He glimpsed the tall bouncer over past the backstage drape, but except that he was uncomfortably near Unity, it didn't matter—the back way was not a way out, having been boarded shut.

Before Ki could get through the throng, the band quit playing and the bouncer spotted him. Ki quickened his pace and began staggering, while the trio put down their instruments, and the bouncer looked peevish but unconcerned, dismissing Ki as just another returning souse. Hastening, Ki blundered past those in his path, grinning blearily at others who laughed and avoided his reeling gait. But he was moving fast for a man in a redeye stupor, and managed to reach the stage a pace behind Unity, who had turned and was starting to walk toward the drape.

He touched her shoulder. Startled, she spun.

"Ki! I thought you'd left to sleep it off."

"The fresh air sobered me up. C'mon, we've got to go."

"You're kidding."

"No, I—"

"Then you're still drunk," she snapped. "Blind drunk. I can't leave dressed like this, don't you see that?"

But Ki wasn't looking at her. He was eyeing the tall bouncer, who'd perked up and was approaching, belligerent now, as though he'd decided that Ki had proven to be a returning pest as well.

"Wear my shirt," Ki said, and took her arm. "Come *on*."

"Try not to leave scars, will you?" she rebuked him scornfully, resisting his tug. It gave the bouncer time to close and block Ki.

"Botherin' the lady again, huh?" the bouncer growled, reaching for Ki. "Let go o' her, dummy, while you're still able to."

Ki saw that the bouncer's move was a grab at his left wrist. He was familiar with that trick, having used a variation earlier on Lloyd, and knew what to expect. Or rather, he knew what the bouncer expected: a quick wrench on the wrist that would whip Ki into an arm-torturing hammerlock, then a bum's rush out of here, with Ki helpless on tiptoe.

"No, don't," Ki quavered, releasing Unity and lifting an apparently awkward, defending arm. The bouncer lunged confidently—and abruptly became acrobatic as Ki's hands fastened around his wrists instead.

"Ki, what're you doing?" Unity cried irately, as

138

the bouncer flew through the air and landed on the table behind them. He split its top and snapped all four legs, scattering glasses and toppling the three men seated there over backwards in their chairs. And Unity's blue eyes were like slivers of dark sapphire. "For God's sake, Ki, stop this, leave me alone—"

His elbow jabbed her in the stomach. All her wind gushed out and she hinged limply into his arms. "A mild attack of the vapors," Ki declared loudly to the crowd, and began hustling her toward the drape. "Needs to rest, is all," he added, glancing around; the tall bouncer was still dazed, but his stocky partner was steaming this way, scowling. "Don't worry, she'll be okay."

"I *am* okay," she wheezed, and slumped against his chest, whimpering despairingly, eyes closed, fighting for breath.

Well, at least she wasn't fighting him now, Ki observed as he held her in his embrace. Still, he felt ashamed of himself for punching a woman, but he hadn't known what else to do—or, come to think of it, where else to go. The back way was a hazard, he knew. But the front way had suddenly become a dead end; to try dragging this hurt, half-nude lady through that saloon crowd would absolutely guarantee his getting mobbed. As it was, the tall bouncer was starting to struggle up from his mortifying setback. The patrons around him were chattering about never having seen him bested before, but never having seen such a toss before, either. And the stocky bouncer was hurtling nearer, aware that unless he avenged his partner, that toss would end their usefulness here. Every other drunk in town would be in trying the same thing.

"Think, Unity, think of a way out," Ki kept urging. They were past the curtain now and coming even with her door. "It can't all be sealed off back here. There's got to be some way out."

"I dunno, I can't think . . ." She raised her face and looked at him, eyes huge and watery. "I don't want

139

anything to do with you!" Stiffening and breaking free, she dashed into her room. "Go away!"

Ki followed, slamming the door behind him. "You must get out of here."

Snatching up her red cape, Unity wrapped it about her bare shoulders as she sagged onto the bed. "Please, stop pestering me," she begged, then straightened suddenly and leaped to her feet with a startled look. "There's something in my bed!" she shrieked, flinging back the covers.

Coiled on her sheet was a four-foot diamondback rattler. Its rattles buzzing, its black tongue flicking, the snake yawned its fanged mouth as it struck at her—

The venomous head toppled off, blood spurting from its severed neck, as Ki spun a *shuriken* to decapitate the deadly reptile.

Ki didn't try to explain; time was too short and her shock was too great. He steered her toward the door, and Unity now shrank willingly against his chest. "There might be a way out, Ki, it's—"

With a screech of ripping hinges, the door burst inward, and the two bouncers bunched together, squeezing and clawing to be the first in. The tall one butted his partner aside and lunged forward.

Ki, having pushed Unity away, was waiting with an odd smile that masked his anger, as the tall bouncer charged, his face purple with fury, and threw a roundhouse right.

Ki blocked the bouncer's punch with his left forearm, while chopping the edge of his right hand down against his nose. The crack of cartilage was audible, and tears welled in the bouncer's eyes, as Ki's left hand slewed around to grip his outflung arm, and Ki's foot hit him in the side of his knee. He folded to one side; Ki dropped with him, kneeling on one knee, and swinging him into a *semo-otoshi*, a kneeling shoulder throw. For the second time, the bouncer sailed over

Ki's head. He came down across the rattler on Unity's bed, his head smacking the wall and knocking him groggy.

Even before his partner hit, the stocky bouncer was driving at Ki, a bone-handled bowie-style knife in his fist. "I'm gonna gut you from gizzard to next Sunday!" he bellowed, slashing.

Ki had already glimpsed the bouncer drawing his knife from a hidden sheath in back of his shirt neck. This was one of the reasons he'd tossed the tall one, for now he was able to lash upward with a high snap-kick. The bouncer caught Ki's heel smack on the chin. Its whipping force was so hard that it jarred the knife loose from his grasp. And Ki, stepping forward with the arc of his kick, grabbed the bouncer's right arm and left shoulder, while slipping his foot in slightly behind one leg. The bouncer, toppling backward from the kick and sideways from Ki's hands, fell into a *hizi-otoshi*, or elbow-drop, as Ki dipped to his right knee and yanked hard.

The bouncer catapulted upside-down through the air, and flattened resoundingly atop his tall partner, collapsing the bed, the snake, and both men to the floor. The stocky bouncer sprawled there, stunned, staring sightlessly into the other's glazed eyes.

Ki pulled Unity from the room. "Where's your way out?"

"Second door, the one painted like the drape," she answered, pointing back up the hallway. "The Entertainment Room, it's called. Some of the girls confided they'd unstuck the window in there, but—"

"Come on, before those fellows wake up." Reaching for her hand, Ki plunged toward the burgundy door. If it was locked, he had his lock picks; if it was bolted, they were dead. But when he tested the door, he wasn't surprised to find that he could edge it open. Even while in use, such "entertainment rooms" stayed unlocked, in case a working girl ran into trouble and needed help fast. Gently, Ki eased the door wider.

"But if it's shut, Ki, it means—"

Ki placed a warning finger to his lips, guided Unity through, then slipped in alongside her and softly closed the door.

"Ah, like this." The voice came from behind an ell in the dark room. It sounded heavy with lust and whiskey, and was accompanied by rhythmically squeaking bedsprings. Francine's voice, Ki recognized wryly. "No, you're missing now. There, that's it, yes..."

Directly across was the window, Ki saw, curtained, its lower sash partially raised. A good thing, and it wasn't a wonder the girls unboarded and opened it, Ki thought; the steamy, sweaty air of the room was more fetid than a swamp. He gave Unity's hand a little nudge, and together they started tiptoeing slowly toward the window.

"Anybody there?" a gruff voice slurred.

They froze. Ki guessed it was one of the miners, who'd gone to bed drunk and was now coming alert, bewildered and confused. Then another voice grumbled, "You're losing the stroke," and Ki grinned. Francine had figured out how to satisfy both miners' appetites.

There was the pop of a cork, the gurgle of a bottle. The springs returned to bouncing. Ki began leading Unity forward again.

Then the bed grew quiet, and they crouched in the darkness, holding their breaths. "What're you up to now?" the second miner growled. The first miner muttered and turned, rumpling bedcovers.

Then Ki heard the click of a gun hammer, and he realized they were in a tight spot. That man had a cocked pistol in hand. He was sitting up, as likely as not, ready to shoot.

Then, out in the hallway, Grantree's ugly, infuriated voice reverberated: "Strauss! Danebo! What in crap are you two assholes lyin' in there for? Get out and find them! They can't have gone far!"

"There, what'd I tell you?" The first miner's voice was still slurred, and he wasn't being very logical, but he was quitting the bed. He started stumbling for the door to the hallway.

The ell blocked the miner's view, but once he got up, he'd spot them. The room was dark, but not pitch black like the office corridor; it was just the dimness of an unlit room, with curtains closed to dusky evening. So Ki glided soundlessly toward the ell, to intercept the miner while he was only half alert and still unaware.

The instant the miner appeared, Ki sprang into a *tobi-geri* leap kick, sailing across and striking the miner in the chest. He purposely restrained his force, so he wouldn't crush ribs or rupture innards, but his stiffened foot still packed enough of a wallop to buckle the miner and send him windmilling backwards, plummeting into the ell.

The heavy roar of a pistol filled the room. A chair or table crashed, then came a thumping and squealing of the bed's rusty casters. There was much thrashing of bedclothes, and a great deal of loud swearing and louder shrieking by Francine, punctuated by more crunching and bumping, as if the ell were a snakepit of writhing bodies.

Ki ran back, grabbed Unity, and they raced for the window. The sash wouldn't budge higher, so Unity crawled under it feet first, clung to the sill with both hands, and dropped. Ki flew headlong through the narrow space as the pistol thundered again, and a bullet punctured the glass pane a few inches above Ki's diving body.

Hitting the ground in a tumble and rolling to his feet, Ki joined Unity in a dashing sprint up the alley to the street.

They kept to the wall, where the shadows lay thickest, and Ki was relieved that this was the alley on the other side of the saloon; they wouldn't have to worry about someone shooting at them from the pantry door. But that didn't stop someone from leaning out the window and shooting at them, missing them in the darkness.

The street would afford little concealment from anybody who might be chasing them, so Ki and Unity cut across it and slipped quickly into another alley. They tore around to the back of an assayer's office, and ran along its rear and those of some shanties, toward a cross-street. They were about to emerge from the alley when Unity, panting, leaned against the wall of a building.

"Wait," she gasped, quivering from exertion. "Must rest . . ."

"Not for long," Ki cautioned, checking around for pursuit. "I don't think Grantree will try shaking the town apart for us, but—"

"You mean he put the snake in my bed?" She shook her head. "Why?"

"I don't know why, but I do mean him." Swiftly Ki told her how he'd overheard Grantree's plot, then he said, "I'm sorry I got rough with you, but I had to get you out."

"And I almost trusted that man," she whispered bleakly, then looked at Ki with eyes an alpine blue. "All right, I'm out. Out of my room, my clothes, my job, and half of my wits. Any suggestions?"

Ki shrugged. "Stay out of his saloon. But as I said, I don't believe Grantree will send men out on a town-wide hunt. His snake trick backfired, but he doesn't know that we know it was meant to kill you, so he'll probably act as though it was an accident. Still, I'm only guessing, so I don't suggest you stake your life on it."

"What can I do?" she began, then stopped. They flattened against the building wall as a couple of tough rowdies stalked down the side-street boardwalk. After they'd gone, Unity shivered and said, "Maybe they're Grantree's goons, maybe not. Where can I go?"

Ki said nothing, sensing that any real offer of help would be taken as charity and refused. At times her independence was a pain in the ass—such as her defiance in the saloon—yet generally Ki liked and admired such fierce streaks of pride in a woman.

"Very well, Ki, if your hotel will let me in like this." Her eyes were a mellower blue now. "I do owe you, don't I?"

Ki grinned, still not relying on words to respond to her. Besides, she'd settled the issue, so far as she was concerned; he'd long ago learned that when an independent woman gave, she gave completely.

Moving on, they sneaked through the rear lanes of Virginia City, constantly darting from dim nook to dark cranny. At last they ventured into the Palace and approached the snotty desk clerk, who frowned at Unity's scanty outfit, but sized up Ki's expression and prudently stifled his observations. He slapped the room key and Jessie's note on the counter, and stared after them indignantly.

Once inside, with the door locked and the lamp lit, Ki told Unity to relax, and made a cursory search of the room. No snakes in the bed or gunmen in the closet, but he found the window unlatched. Fixing that, he stood reading Jessie's message then gazed out at the night.

Unity said, "I relax better with my clothes off."

Turning from the window, Ki saw that her cape, skirt, and boots were heaped carelessly on the floor. Unity was now completely naked. She was stretching her arms, a kittenish smile perking her lips.

"Come on, Ki. What are you waiting for?"

She fastened her eyes provocatively upon him while he stripped, as if she had waited impatiently all day to get a peek at his nude masculinity. Then, teasingly grasping Ki by his erect member, she led him to the bed, where they lay down together in a heated embrace.

Ki had traveled similar erotic routes with independent women, and true to type, Unity did not care for coyness or prolonged buildups. Hers was an elemental need, and once she made up her mind, she pursued her target with a minimum of ruffles and flourishes. At times Ki preferred the no-nonsense approach— such as now, when, having gone through that tense, prolonged battle at the Silverado, he had little energy and less desire for appetizers or spectacular productions.

He cupped her breasts and sucked one of her nipples into his mouth. She acted as though she expected him to bite it, but in a moment she was stroking his hair and pushing him closer, and Ki knew she liked the sensation of it. He suckled on both her breasts until, wriggling, she crushed herself along his body, and he could feel her eager strength throbbing in heat along the entire length of him.

Unity wrapped one leg over him, then hesitated, drawing in her breath. Her gentle yet insistent pressure was a hint that Ki could accept or reject. With an inward smile, he accepted and turned over onto his back. Unity then raised herself and squatted over him, astride his pelvis with her knees on the bed on either side of his hips. There, gazing down at him with eyes of passion, she rose and impaled herself on his spear, contracting her strong thighs so that the muscular action clamped her passage tightly around his rigid manhood.

Ki clenched his buttocks, thrusting his hips off the bed. Unity spread her thighs so that, sliding up and down, she soon contained the whole of his shaft in her squeezing loins. Her head sagged forward, then was flung back in arousal, her mouth open and gasping, her eyes squeezed tightly shut, her long wheat-golden hair swaying and brushing down over her shoulders and across his chest.

Ki grasped her jiggling breasts, toying with them until she bent to kiss him. Then again she arched up and back as she plunged like the rider of a bucking

146

bronco. He pumped up into her with deeper and faster strokes. Her thighs descended with increasing force, as if each time she were collapsing on the downward surge—only to revive just in time to draw her plundered belly up on his erection yet again . . . and again . . .

Ki, tensing upward, felt the gripping of her loins tearing at his entrails, and he clasped her waist and penetrated her to the hilt. And her passage kept squeezing, milking, until he felt himself bursting, spurting far up into her, while her own face contorted and twisted in fiery orgasm.

Then, with a deep sigh, Unity crouched limp and satisfied over Ki. Slowly, sighing contentedly, she eased off his passive body and moved up slightly to stretch languidly beside him. Finally she stirred and caressed his cheek, while Ki just lay there vanquished.

"Guess I should say thanks, Ki. Well, I do say it." Slowly she swung up to sit cross-legged on the covers. "This doesn't happen very often with me, Ki. I'm not one of Grantree's girls. I'm worse. I'm a cheat who seems to give but only takes. There are times I hope I can become more like them, giving an honest dollar's worth. But I can't even give that. I'm beyond hope."

"Cheer up. Hope makes the world spin."

"Funny, my father used to say love did it. But I couldn't plan on that, either. Now I don't plan, I just take it a day at a time."

"No other plans at all?"

"Oh, the Monteplata. It's the only home I've got now, I guess, and nobody's going to scare me out of it." She paused and turned moody. "I haven't any idea what Grantree's up to, what all this bad business is about." She flattened her hands over her face. When she lowered them again, she looked frightened. "Ki, what am I going to do?"

Ki silenced her with a finger to her lips. "Take it a night at a time," he replied gently, and tugged her back into his arms.

147

★

Chapter 14

As soon as was practical the following morning, Ki
and Unity left the hotel and rode hard for Noah
Winthrop's sheep ranch. It was still well before noon
when, entering the wide lodgepole-fenced yard, they
reined in by the front porch of the ranchhouse.

Noah Winthrop opened the door. "Why, Unity,
that you?"

"Sure is, Mr. Winthrop. Do you know Ki?"

"I do now," Winthrop drawled, shaking hands. "I
was told to expect you, Ki, and Unity's a guest
anytime." He ushered them toward the kitchen. "I'll
brew some coffee. Gabe an' Miss Starbuck drank a
whole pot, just since they arrived here 'bout dawn."

"About dawn, was it?" Unity echoed, ten degrees
cooler.

This brief exchange made Ki realize that Unity
cared for Gabe more than she was willing to admit.
Gabe's feelings were less well suppressed; he bolted

148

to his feet from where he and Jessie were seated at the kitchen table.

"Unity! What'n glory are you—ah, what a great surprise!"

Jessie's greeting held a tone of relief and welcome. "I was becoming worried, Ki, that maybe something had happened to you."

"No, we were delayed a bit, buying supplies." Ki handed Jessie her note-map and a telegram. "This wire came for you."

Mentally decoding its message, Jessie stiffened, then shook her head to warn Ki not to say more. But the others weren't paying attention. Noah Winthrop was fixing coffee, while Gabe eyeballed Unity pirouetting in her new denim pants, man's-style plaid shirt, and calfskin vest.

Sweetly she said, "And Ki was so kind to buy them for me."

"Wha-a-t?" Gabe cried. But he settled down, listening attentively with Jessie to Ki's account of what had led up to Unity's refitting.

"So you see," Ki finished, "Unity couldn't go back to her room, and we decided she'd be safer here, out of town and not left alone."

"A snake, huh? And Grantree could've passed it off as an accident, too. The country's teeming with rattlers." Gabe took Unity's hand. "I'm sure glad you took her under your wing, Ki."

A wing wasn't all she'd been under, Jessie suspected, and swiftly, before Gabe got around to wondering where Unity had spent the night, she said, "A piece of good news. We now know Mastleg didn't steal all those sheep." Then, while the coffee came to a boil, she told all—well, almost all—that had happened to her and Gabe.

"But if my stepfather didn't do it," Unity said, "who did? Ghosts? I mean, how could they spirit out through the east cliff of the valley?"

"That remains to be seen," Jessie replied thought-

149

fully. "Ki, I'd like to ride out that way and try to pick up their tracks."

"Ghosts don't leave tracks," Gabe interjected. "You'll be taking a ride for nothing."

After coffee, however, Gabe insisted on accompanying Jessie and Ki; and since he was going, Unity refused to stay behind. Gabe also provided them two of the ranch's Spencer carbines and saddle boots—"Just as a precaution," he explained. "Nothin's likely to happen in broad daylight, but after last night, I'm taking no chances."

Shortly the four were riding slowly eastward, past the scene of the previous night's gunfight. Ki stayed close to where Jessie and Gabe said the raiders had fled, his keen gaze intently searching the ground. A few miles farther on, in the cliff face ahead they could see the shadowy slit of a narrow cut. Its floor was hard and stony, thinly grown with brush except along the walls. At its entrance, Ki found a few barely tangible signs of animals having come and gone.

"Not that it means much," Ki commented. "Chances are they were looking for water back in there. The faintest scent will do it."

"'Cept it's bone dry," Gabe retorted laconically.

"Then they had other reasons. Or maybe they're horses whose riders had reasons." Ki smiled tautly and veered into the cut, which slashed the hills in a northerly direction. "Let's make sure."

They rode on, intent and watchful, but the scraggly grass showed no marks of passing hooves. Once, however, Ki's quick glance noted a fresh white score on a slab of rock, the kind of scrape made by the iron of a shod horse. It gave them a needed boost, but after another fifteen minutes they abruptly reined in and stared.

Gabe swore under his breath, "Goddamn, I tried to tell him."

Directly ahead was a sheer rock wall sloping up

against the blue of the late-morning sky. The draw was like all the others, a box.

"It was a nice idea," Jessie consoled, "but it appears this really is only a blind alley for straying animals, after all."

"Must be. No animal I ever heard of could get up that rock, and the side walls are just as steep," Unity agreed, sighing.

Ki sat frowning at the blank wall. "Those marks back there didn't look like the prints of strays," he insisted. "And that horseshoe scratch looked fresh."

He jiggered his horse toward the east wall of the draw, and rode slowly back the way they had come, examining the rock wall for some fissure he might have missed on his first go-round.

The other three trailed behind, depressed by the rearing cliffs and the thick, tall scrub that grew like a fringe along the stony base. They appreciated Ki's perseverance, but thought he was pursuing a lost cause. The close, bristly growth stretched unmarred, untouched by any passing animal, and the rock wall continued, looming unbroken back to the valley.

Suddenly Ki halted again, his eyes narrowing. The stretch of brush he was just passing stood straight and tall, but there was a withered look about the leaves on the topmost branches, a tinge of yellow at variance with the fresh green of the shrubbery on either side. For perhaps a dozen feet this peculiar manifestation seemed apparent to him.

Dismounting, Ki approached the growth, broke off a branch of one of the bushes, and snapped it sharply between his fingers. "Dry," he said, turning to the others. "Do you see that? Dry and dead."

Gabe slipped from his saddle, seized the gnarled trunk of another bush with both hands, and tugged sharply. The trunk tore easily out of the ground; it had no roots. Now Jessie and Unity joined in, yanking on shrubs and wrenching them free, finding that these too had bases that had been crudely axed to form sharpened stakes. Within minutes they had made a gap in the growth a couple of yards in width. Through it shone the cliff wall, and the mouth of a cave.

Wordlessly they regarded the dark hole, as Ki grinned with satisfaction.

"An old trick," Jessie said after a moment. "But a good one. Cut out the brush, then stick it in the ground after you pass through the gap. That way there are no broken branches or trampled growth."

"I gotta admit, I've ridden up in here a time or two, and never suspected the cave was here," Gabe said. "I reckon nobody would notice the break in the bushes, 'less they were looking might sharp."

"And had a notion of what to look for," Unity added.

"Well, I wouldn't have seen it if whoever did it hadn't gotten careless and neglected to replace the withered bushes with fresh ones," Ki allowed. He went to his horse, rummaged through the supplies he'd bought, and returned to pass around four large miner's candles. "It's dark in there, and the going is apt to be rough."

After lighting their candles, they walked their horses into the cave. Its sides were smooth and water-worn, its floor carpeted with fine silt sprinkled with pebbles and small, rounded boulders. It was too low-ceilinged to mount up, so they continued afoot, leading their horses, though the floor had a slight slope and was devoid of pitfalls.

Unity exclaimed, "Why, this must be a tunnel, boring right on through the hill to a canyon or gorge. The silt's full of tracks!"

Jessie nodded. "I'd guess this is the old bed of a stream that once ran through here a very, *very* long time ago, when this area was different from the way it is now."

For some time they moved on through the bleak darkness that was relieved only by their flickering candle flames. Eventually they glimpsed light ahead, and five minutes later they were mounting their horses outside the far mouth of the tunnel. Before them angled a narrow gorge trending in a northerly direction. Up its middle ran a bare-earth pathway that showed evidence of recent travel.

"Well, we found the sheep run," Gabe declared angrily, after they'd sat viewing the gorge awhile. He wheeled his horse toward the tunnel. "Didn't take much, a few withered leaves. But it's enough, I swear, for us Winthrops to put the screws on some slippery thieves."

"Good," Jessie said with approval. "You and Unity go get the ranch crew, while Ki and I take a *pasear* to visit Doc Everard's camp."

Gabe frowned. "I still believe the lawyer's fed you a yarn. That area's never panned out for mining, only for attracting scroungers after the train loot, it bein' near where the bandits held out."

"Maybe so, Gabe. But true or not, Neville had his reasons for saying so, and I want to try finding out what they are."

Gabe eyed Jessie thoughtfully. "Could be worth it," he conceded, and pointed up the gorge. "Take it up till you hit a trail, then cut east and just follow your map. You'll be on the cutoff Neville drew, not too far from the canyons." He turned to Unity. "Might as well go. Pa and my brothers will be chomping at the bit to put in on this."

Unity hesitated. "I think we all should—"

"No," Ki interrupted firmly. "You know where we're heading. The sooner you can get back here with help, the better."

With a final worried glance at Jessie and Ki, Unity allowed Gabe to relight their candles, then lead the way back into the tunnel.

Ki waited until their hoofbeats had faded, then said, "You can't mean to follow the map, Jessie, not after reading your telegram. Neville's a part-time cartel lawyer and a full-time crook, disbarred and jailed in

Montana for theft, and he was in Deer Lodge at the same time as Everard. He must be setting a trap for us."

She nodded, smiling. "The wire was news, all right, but it only confirmed my suspicions. You see, I think he figured we wouldn't believe his crazy story, but it would goad us into checking his map anyway."

"I don't get it. Why let him believe we'd fall for it?"

"Ki, if it was simply a trap, Neville could've sent us directly to Everard's claim, right?" Jessie's smile broadened. "My hunch is there's something he doesn't want seen there, and he wants us out of the way before we start snooping. So, while he or whoever works for him is out of the way, waiting to trap us, we'll go snoop first."

"One thing's certain, we won't be able to do it afterwards," Ki objected, and heeled his horse up the gorge.

Mile after mile they rode, north of the confines of the sheep valley. At one point they came upon a multitude of sheep and horse prints, where a small rivulet formed a patch of soggy ground. The marks continued up the gorge, and the ground firmed up again, becoming a hard and rocky floor upon which hooves left no sign at all. A mile or so after that, the gorge intersected a hollow, through which sliced a trail.

Turning right, they let their horses pick their own pace as the trail ascended the hollow, skirted some forested banks, and curved among a series of gaps and tables. Recalling Gabe's words about the train robbers having held off the posse somewhere around here, Jessie tried to visualize the area through an outlaw's eyes. The trail would be a dream for an outlaw; if pursuit became too hot, he'd be able to leave the trail and strike out to either side, where he'd be swallowed up by forest.

The sun was well past its zenith when the trail

capped a knoll and lazily declined southeastward along meadowed steppes. Reining in where the trail crossed by the mouth of a wide, inviting canyon, Jessie consulted Neville's map, then rose in her stirrups to peer down the trail. Between one and two miles farther on, she could just make out the dark, narrow streak of a second canyon entrance.

"This ought to be the one to Everard's claim," she said, and cut toward the canyon, sliding her carbine out of its sheath.

Ki also carried his carbine in the open, as they entered the canyon and rode down its center. Gradually the sides closed in, becoming more weathered and rotten, with numerous blotches of deserted mine burrows. The canyon eventually funneled into what was virtually a ravine, an elongated bottleneck that stretched some distance ahead before widening back out again.

Restlessly they trotted deeper through the narrow cut. Jessie kept her gaze roving, while Ki's eyes remained fixed almost hypnotically on the looming crags that flanked them like jagged balustrades.

Suddenly Ki stiffened. A man had appeared on the canyon rim, running parallel to them, stopping, stooping, and then running again. Ki shouldered and fired his carbine, its report bouncing deafeningly from the walls. The man stooped again, and yet again darted forward. Ki's second shot thundered, and the man pitched down out of sight.

"Ride!" Ki yelled, kicking his horse. "Ride, Jessie!"

A huge explosion rocked the canyon. Jessie turned in her saddle and glanced up behind Ki as they raced in headlong flight. A puff of dust and smoke hung over the cliffs they'd just passed, as tons of earth and massive boulders avalanched down to engulf the canyon floor, eye-stabbing grit surging at them in a stifling cloud. A second, closer explosion jarred them,

155

almost panicking their galloping horses. Another shower of broken rock spurted from a point opposite them and halfway to the rim.

Ahead the canyon widened, but that refuge might have been a dozen miles away, for all the safety it afforded. They both were well aware that in ambushes like this, a third powder blast could be expected to come from in front, timed to catch their escape.

Nonetheless, they yelled and lashed their mounts into a frenzied and convulsive effort, though the quaking ground broke their stride. Smaller rocks rolled past them, but miraculously missed their horses' flashing legs. And as the detonations and concussions died to a heavy rumbling of echoes, they realized they'd apparently been spared that final, assuredly fatal blast. But they didn't pause until they reached the place where the canyon began widening, and then they slowed to a halt and looked.

There was no more canyon behind them. Even through the dust cloud, they could see that it was now filled halfway to the rim with a great pile of boulders and earth. Stones and dirt still rattled down, and a look upward showed them tons of overhanging rim, partly loosened and poised to fall at the slightest nudge.

"You saved our lives, Ki," Jessie said, her voice still shaky. "Your second shot either wounded or killed that man. Whichever, it prevented him from setting off any more dynamite."

Watching the rim, Ki responded with more calmness than he felt. "It took some planning to rig those blasts properly. Neville must've started last night. Jessie, how was he so sure we'd come this way?"

"Perhaps he wasn't, and that man you shot was our already dead Everard, protecting his claim against trespassers." Jessie laughed ruefully. "Or perhaps Neville was sure, which means I didn't fool him for one holy second. He figured that I'd use his story as an excuse to search the claim, and arranged accordingly. Then again, perhaps not, and he's also posted a trap in the other canyon as well."

"And they say Orientals are inscrutable," Ki snorted. "Well, ghosts don't use dynamite any more than they leave tracks, so this has to be Neville's tricky figuring. Maybe with the cave-in, he'll assume his trap worked, and we'll have time to explore the claim."

"Perhaps Neville's figured a trick to cover that too. His shyster's brain seems to work as fast and straight as your carbine, Ki."

★

Chapter 15

Once the canyon began widening, its sides continued a gradual leaning away and lowering as well. Only once, sharply and briefly, did they draw close together again, and then they seemed to converge almost into one unbroken cliff. It was there, in a small pocket clearing, that Jessie and Ki located Everard's leased mining claim.

The pocket's north wall was the base of a towering hill, with a ledge slanted upward from the canyon floor. It was used to form a footing for the heavily timbered mine entrance, which was barely as high as a man's head, and not more than three feet wide. A landslide had closed much of the entrance, but along one edge a small boulder had held back the dirt and exposed the black opening to the tunnel.

Before climbing to the drift entrance, they made a quick tour of the pocket. The few old shanties and shacks still standing were empty and decayed, and all the equipment, except for a few broken hand tools, was gone. They could discover no sign that the claim had been visited in the recent past, though from just below the drift, ruts of a wagon trail still gouged faint, spidery lines eastward along the canyon floor.

When they hiked up to the mine entrance, however, there was spoor. In the soft dirt were many tracks, though none appeared fresh. Almost at once Ki noticed a significant peculiarity about them: they all headed into the tunnel, but none headed out. It was as though everyone who'd last entered the mine had somehow managed to perish inside.

They relit their candles and, stooping, squeezed through the opening into the musty tunnel. As they advanced along the shored-up drift, they passed cross-tunnels with old tracks leading into each of these, and then returning. The tracks in the main passage lured them on, deeper toward the heart of the surrounding hill. Soon the drift swung sharply northward, and shortly after that, the lagging above them and the timbers shoring the sides became fresher and less rotted. This was the portion of the mine last worked, they realized; the answer to the tracks lay somewhere up ahead.

Suddenly Ki's candle shone on a sloping wall in their way. He held the candle higher, advancing cautiously. "It's completely blocked, Jessie," he said, and bent to examine the floor. "And here, the footsteps disappear right underneath the rockfall."

But something on the right wall attracted Jessie's attention. She moved over and held her light higher, close to the wall. She discovered that she was staring at a spot where a small hole had been bored into the tunnel.

"Well, here's an unused drill hole," she said. "A manmade cave-in. Whoever did the blasting was caught and never got out."

Ki was noncommittal, not totally convinced of this evident explanation as they started back toward the entrance. Once he imagined he heard tapping somewhere, as though men imprisoned under that slide were trying to dig their way free. Yet he knew this was foolish; those tracks were months old, and any men buried there would long since have died.

They reached the bend in the drift and saw the little gray patch ahead indicating the entrance. Gradually it became larger and brighter, with afternoon sunlight slanting in a few feet. When they came to the light and blew out their candles, Jessie paused, then clutched Ki's arm.

"It just occurred to me, Ki; my candle flame wavered, bent toward me when I held it close to look at that drill hole. It means there must be a current of air flowing out through that hole."

Ki mulled that over for a moment, then grinned and patted her hand. "It means more than that, Jessie. It means the tunnel goes all the way through, but those men who made the tracks blocked it behind them so nobody could follow. They're working from the north slope of the hill; that tapping I thought was imagination was their picking."

"They wouldn't have gone to such trouble without good cause. Or bad cause." Jessie pursed her lips, then continued, "Now all we've got to do is ride around over there and look for the other end of this."

"We could follow that faint wagon trail," Ki suggested. "It could be that those men used it to transfer their mining equipment."

Riding out of the pocket, they headed along the canyon, with the shadowy bulk of the hill on their left. As the canyon continued on its easterly course, the hill curved more toward the north. Soon the narrow sides expanded again, the canyon evolving into a valley with gradually sloping sides. Ki had been growing increasingly uneasy, and by the time they reached a low spot in the valley slopes, he was often glancing backwards. When they came to a much clearer trail branching northwestward, circling back toward the

160

hill, they halted to look at the trail, and Jessie asked him why he was so restless.

"Just a feeling, Jessie. Neville's too crafty not to lay two traps for us, one in each canyon. Whoever's at the second would have heard the explosions and rushed over. If the man I shot was only wounded, or if somebody's got the wits to see that the third charge didn't detonate, we could have company coming fast behind us."

"Well, what do you want to do?"

"Take the trail, of course." Ki grinned and leaned over to examine it. "It looks well traveled from here in both directions. I guess that's why Neville mapped the other way in, so we wouldn't see this."

"And why, since they don't use the way we came, he figured he could afford to blow the canyon down on us back there," Jessie added. "Well, let's make sure we see them before they see us."

They turned onto the trail, constantly surveying the terrain ahead, on both sides, and behind. Soon heavy brush flanked the trail, obscuring details, and as they approached the hill again, boulders and large stone slabs crowded the trail. They were coming to a short, corrugated rise, when the trail abruptly forked, one branch angling away from the rise, the other continuing straight toward the hill.

They reined in and gazed around slowly before making a decision. Their attention almost immediately centered on the face of the hill and the changes that had appeared in its contour. No more than a quarter of a mile away, a vast sheet of cliff spired upward. It appeared not to be a flat plane, but a deeply curved bay, as if some giant with a scoop had carved a piece neatly out of the slope.

"That's where the tunnel comes out," Jessie cried suddenly. "There's where this trail ahead ends, and where they're mining now."

"Listen," Ki warned.

The rataplan of galloping horses, many of them, sounded along the trail behind them. Praying that her deduction about the trails was correct, Jessie goaded her horse along the leftward-angling branch. Hoping she was, and thus the riders would take the branch straight ahead, Ki veered off after her. They rode fast until they were out of sight of the fork, and then reined in. The drumming hoofbeats drew near, then gradually faded.

"Thank God," she sighed. "Where does this lead?"

"We'll see," Ki said, and nosed his mount forward. The path meandered awhile, then ascended a gentle slope toward an aspen-crowned ridge.

At the crest of the ridge they stopped and stared down into a small hollow below. Nearly a score of sheep grazed on the grass bordering a mountain spring. Jessie laughed and clapped her hands.

"The stolen sheep, Ki! They've been feeding the miners!"

Ki chuckled with her, then looked up at the sun slanting down the western sky. "They'll keep, Jessie. We've got work to do."

They headed back down the path, toward the fork in the trail. When they reached it, they didn't turn onto the other branch, but plunged into the brush toward the higher slopes of the hill. Soon their course brought them to a little open glade, where they dismounted and ground-tied their horses. The furrowing walls of the cliff reared above them to their right. Unsheathing their carbines, Jessie and Ki started hiking toward the precipice. When finally they came to the edge of the cliff, they knelt down in the concealing brush and stared at what lay in the open beyond.

Near the center of the cliff was the dark maw of the mine entrance. Spreading out below it like a huge ramp were the cleared remnants of a rockslide, with a log pile on one side and a mound of tailings on the other. Next to the tailings was a shack for the rock crusher and sluice pump, and a short distance beyond

162

that were sheds and new log cabins facing the inward-curving cliff. A couple of the cabins looked to be bunkhouses, while the longest one had to be the cookshack and mess hall. Around them milled upwards of a dozen men, many with horses—the riders they'd heard. Farther back were a few parked ore wagons, and behind them was a horse corral, built in among the trees.

Jessie asked, "Can you see Neville down there?"

"Not without binoculars."

"Then let's go get a better look."

Cautiously they inched their way into the open, following the base of the high cliff, crouching low and taking such advantage as they could of whatever scant cover was available.

A sudden darting motion by the mess hall drew their attention. A man hurried around from the cookshack side and began beating a large iron triangle. From all sides, men started flowing toward the hall, while others groped their way out of the tunnel and filed down the rockslide.

"What a break," Jessie murmured. "While they're all in one place in there, let's take a quick gander through the hall's rear window, there. I want to know if Neville—or Everard—is here."

When it appeared that everyone was inside the hall, and the last man had closed the door behind him, Jessie and Ki moved again. Creeping silently, careful not to dislodge a loose stone or snap a brittle twig, they stole to within twenty yards of the hall's rear.

The remaining distance was all open ground, though. They angled toward the blind side of a bunkhouse that ran the way they wanted to go, and would favor them with a much shorter stretch of exposure. They advanced along the wall of the bunkhouse, under the shadow of the eaves, almost crawling by the time they reached the corner.

A man swept around the corner and collided with Ki. He was startled, but rebounded instantly; despite

163

his bandaged face and puffy, mottled eyes, he was immediately recognizable as Lloyd. Being Lloyd, he immediately recognized Ki, and drew.

Lloyd was fast. He'd been born with the skill, had practiced it diligently, and had the confidence to use it effectively. He also had his quick-draw holster, which practically fed the butt of his Remington into his palm if he so much as flicked his wrist.

He fired twice, but the second shot was pure reflex; he was already dead. Both shots sailed off harmlessly into the sky as he went over backwards with the handle of Ki's slim *tanto* blade protruding from the loose flesh beneath his chin. Ki had been just a bit faster, stepping forward just as Lloyd drew, bringing the point of the knife upward with savage force, plunging it through muscle, tendon, and bone, and into the gunslinger's brain stem. As Lloyd hit the ground on his back, Ki moved in. Placing a foot squarely in Lloyd's face for leverage, he pulled out the blade. Jessie winced and turned away.

"I guess that proves it," Ki said as he wiped the blade on Lloyd's shirt and then resheathed it. "With Lloyd here, this has to be the hideout of the Posse Comitatus."

From inside the mess hall came a confusion of voices and a clatter of running footsteps. Immediately, Jessie and Ki started at a run for the nearest place they could make a stand—the mine entrance.

They reached the lower end of the crusher shack, and put it between them and their pursuers. Then, lunging up the sloping rockslide, they made a third of the distance before the first shot came. It clipped Jessie's sleeve, and she shied, looking back over her shoulder, only to trip and sprawl forward, clutching her carbine to keep it from being knocked loose. The fall saved her life, for a veritable hail of gunfire swept above them as Ki also dropped to hug the rocks.

On hands and knees, Jessie swiveled around and triggered her carbine. A thin yell drifted up at her, and the men paused in their firing. She got to her feet and, with Ki alongside, raced up the slope toward the shelter of the tunnel in a low-crouching scramble. More rifle and pistol fire chased them now, splintering the thick support beams and whining deep into the tunnel, as they plunged through the entrance.

"I'll check, you cover!" Ki shouted, and before Jessie could answer, he had sprinted past, cat-footed, to see who was in back.

She pivoted and bellied down on the entrance floor, sighting her carbine. Below, a half-dozen men with drawn guns were charging up the slope toward the crusher shack, converging on the mine opening. Behind them swarmed others, one of whom snapped up his rifle and fired a chance shot. It came close, the lead whispering by her ear.

Then she began to fire, feeling the recoil in her shoulder and hearing the metallic clack as she levered in a fresh round. She measured her dwindling shots, forcing the gunmen to dive for shelter, stalling their attack. One lay in the open and did not move. Jessie aimed again, and another of the Posse failed to reach shelter. She swung the muzzle and targeted the body of a man leaping for the tailings mound. She fired, and the man moved three more staggering steps forward before collapsing on his face and lying still.

Answering lead began to reach for her as the Posse riddled the tunnel mouth with volley after volley.

From his shelter behind the crusher shack, one of the Posse shouted orders to some of the men behind him. A jabbering reply that sounded like agreement came from one of the others, and four of them hastened to one of the toolsheds beyond a bunkhouse. When they reappeared, each carried a partially filled gunnysack, and then, splitting into pairs, they began to dash for the base of the rockslide at opposite ends, two toward the log pile, and two for the tailings mound.

The other gunmen broke out with a renewed concentration of gunfire, while Jessie trained on the four, triggering and levering another cartridge from magazine to chamber.

Ki returned from his reconnaissance of the tunnel and slewed in beside her, searching for targets.

"Those two pair, coming from either side! They're carrying dynamite in those bags!" As she spoke, Jessie fired twice more. One of the four fell over his gunnysack. "If even one gets to the cliff, he'll be out of our range, and one stick tossed in here . . ."

She left the obvious unspoken, flipping the lever and pressing the trigger once more. The firing pin came down on an empty chamber. She dropped the carbine and drew her pistol, while Ki tracked and fired, downing another. A third man stumbled but kept crawling, almost getting over the log pile before Ki blew the back of his head off.

And the fourth man reached the cliff. The Posse below cheered him on, pouring raking gunfire into the mine entrance. Jessie and Ki moved to the best possible points from which to shoot, ignoring the searing ricochets as they tried to pick off the surviving dynamiter. But their efforts were not enough. Pressed flat against the cliff face, the man could advance stealthily toward the tunnel mouth without fear that they'd be able to hit him except by stepping outside, which would be sheer suicide.

"We'll have to fall back, Ki," Jessie cried.

Ki shook his head. "It'd be a waste of time. Besides, we may have a chance, if the man out there didn't think to bring a rope."

"A rope! I'm not worried about any rope! The dynamite—"

"And how is he going to throw it in here? With a rope, unless he wasn't smart enough to bring one, and then he'll throw by hand."

Before Jessie could ask more, Ki handed her his carbine and squirreled across to the far side. Easing upright, pressing flat against the tunnel wall, he tried

166

to become as thin as possible to avoid the barrage of bullets bracketing the tunnel mouth.

Then, as if to answer Jessie, the firing tapered off. And she realized that the man must not have a rope; he'd have to get within throwing range, and they'd have to slack off or hit him. And Ki—

Ki was gone. Before the last bullet cracked, he'd launched himself out of the tunnel. For a split second he was in full view of the Posse below, who were expectantly regrouping in a surging mass up the rockslide. He was also glimpsed by the man with the dynamite, who was poised in an awkward, one-legged stance to pitch. He faced Ki from all of four feet away, the gunnysack bunched in his belt, a lighted match in one hand, and a dynamite stick in the other, its fuse sputtering and throwing off sparks.

It was his final conscious sensation.

He never did see the blur of Ki's hands as three *shuriken* winked in the sunlit air. He died before the visual message could reach his brain, blood jetting from his heart, right lung, and throat. From below, the gunmen were already unleashing a withering torrent. Lead thudded into timbers and sprayed biting stone fragments around Ki as, the instant the third *shuriken* left his fingertips, he dove back inside the mine. And the man, arms vainly clenching his chest, hinged forward with the dynamite folded in his death's embrace, and rolled down the slope.

Initially the gunmen were so intent upon slaughtering Ki that they didn't pay much attention to the man tumbling into their midst. When belatedly they did, even the most courageous of them reeled and began scattering and retreating. The carbine blasts from inside the tunnel mouth ripped into them—

Then the one stick of dynamite exploded, detonating the other sticks the man had been carrying. The earth shook, and the gunmen and a large section of the rockpile were swallowed in flame and smoke.

After a moment, debris began pelting down, including grisly chunks of flesh and bone.

The tunnel entrance was an inferno. The air turned acrid, and powder fumes strangled the lungs. Queer, invisible hands plucked at their clothing, yet Ki managed to yell through his choking, "Get set, Jessie! They should be charging us any moment now."

But as the billowing clouds dissipated, they saw that the surviving thugs were breaking for their horses. The toll was too great; it had been too large already, but this dynamite disaster was more than they were being paid to buck. The slope and field were dotted with dead and dying men. Those who turned and fled had to leap clear of the carnage.

"Sort of fitting," Jessie said when things grew quiet again. "The rats were caught in their own trap."

Ki stared down, then gazed at the sky before turning to her. "We've got time. Come here, Jessie, I want to show you something."

She followed Ki some fifty yards into the tunnel, until they came to a small ore cart turned on its side. A glowing Dietz Buckeye safety lantern rested on the dented side, and its load of ore had spilled out. Mixed in with the ore were the bodies of two men. Both had their revolvers drawn, but had fresh knife wounds; Ki had been a shade faster, and a lot deadlier.

"There're a few more I ran into further back," Ki said, bending to pick up a chunk of ore, "but that's not what I want to show you." Using the sharp edge of the cart, he scraped at the ore sample until a cleaned section of it shone bright yellow in the lamplight.

Jessie gasped. "Gold!"

"Refined gold, not raw." Ki placed the chunk in her palm. "This is how gold looks when it's made into bullion."

★

Chapter 16

The shadows were lengthening, and crimson streaked the western horizon as Jessie and Ki left Noah Winthrop's sheep ranch.

Earlier, when they'd been on their way back from the mine, they'd met up with the Winthrop clan and crew, who'd been searching for them. Escorted to the ranch, they ate a quick dinner while their horses rested, and then set out for Virginia City. Unity and Gabe remained behind, after stiff argument. But the discovered mine on her property made Unity's safety all the more crucial, and if the remaining Posse members attempted a retaliatory raid on the ranch, Gabe's gun hand would be sorely needed.

Riding hurriedly away, Jessie and Ki paused at the edge of the ranch to wave, then went on at a more leisurely pace to conserve their horses' energies. Hours later, when they arrived in town, the surrounding slopes had darkened from gray to hard cobalt, and the glazed eyes of windows glowed a lambent yellow, with only the marshal's office appearing to be entirely lightless.

Dismounting, Ki muttered a curse. "Damn, he's out again."

"Likely making his rounds," Jessie said, equally frustrated. "Well, we'll just have to go find him—or his deputy."

Tying their horses to the rail, they continued afoot so Ki could check inside the packed saloons and dance halls. They peered into black alleyways and scanned the swarming boardwalks and street traffic, but for a distressing long while they failed to catch a glimpse, a voice, or any indication of a lawman. When finally they did, it was not what they expected.

Jessie spotted Tilden first. He was far in the next block, pushing through the crowd away from them; and he was flanked, she saw with a start, by Grantree and Chester Neville.

The three men turned the corner. Jessie and Ki hurried to catch up, but when they reached the corner, they saw only Neville. He was standing at the corner ahead, his hands in his pockets, staring thoughtfully along the intersecting street.

Jessie began, "Now, where did they—"

"Probably to the Silverado, if Tilden's stayed with Grantree," Ki ventured. "Anyway, that's the direction Neville's looking in."

"Something's strange. Certainly one of the surviving Posse members, at least, would've gotten here by now and tipped off Grantree."

"Or Neville."

"All right, both. They should be skipping town, instead of chumming with the law." She paused as Neville started walking away, then said, "Ki, you go on after Tilden. I'll follow Neville."

"But—"

"Hurry!" Jessie was already on her way, sidestepping people where possible, and jostling others who refused to make way.

Soon she had the lawyer in view, and dogged his

heels while he headed uphill toward his house. The traffic thinned, so she slowed and let him gain some distance in case he chanced to look back. Keeping well back in the shadows of residences, she continued to trail him, excitement whipping her nerves. Neville was up to more trickery, she sensed, and she was not about to let him slip away or rig another trap.

Ki turned toward the Silverado, concerned about Jessie's safety, and hoping he'd quickly overtake the marshal. Grantree could be a problem if he was still with him, but of primary importance was informing Tilden and having the official word spread. Until then, Grantree and Neville merely needed to wipe out Jessie, himself, and a small sheepherding operation, to retain their secret and restore their gang.

Thinking of this made Ki wonder just how many of the Posse were on the loose, and how many had fled here to town. The noisy swirl of people helped to conceal him, but it also hid from him any peril that might be lurking in it.

The sense of something strange, something wrong, grew stronger as he approached the Silverado. Its colorful façade was unlit, its entrance torches doused, and no music or hilarity filtered out from behind its closed doors. Standing in front were the pirate doorman and Ki's two favorite bouncers, stolidly waving away any customers.

Without the Silverado's light, the street and boardwalk were peculiarly dark. There was nothing to indicate the existence of hidden men, but Ki's acute instincts detected their presence. Advancing, he heard Grantree's loud voice: "... gal covering us while her Chink friend vamoosed. Your deputy's lying where he plugged him."

The saloon owner and the marshal were about abreast of the alleyway on this side, Ki judged. He could just manage to make them out where they came to a pause on the boardwalk, as Tilden spoke up: "I still don't cotton to you putting out all your lights."

"Pandemonium, Fritz. Panic reigned supreme afterwards, and I thought it best to close for the night, despite the personal cost." Grantree stopped, his head thrusting toward Ki like that of a turtle. Then he exploded, "The son of a bitch is back, Fritz! It's him!"

Ki halted, quiet and motionless. Grantree, swift for his bulk, dove through the entrance door. The marshal remained, and he must not have seen Ki, for he kept peering, turning slowly. "What's plaguing you now, Grantree? Where'd you go? *Who's* back?"

"Bonehead, your deputy's killer is comin' at you!" Grantree shouted from the doorway, then bawled an order: "Hit it, boys!"

Ki leaped away as pistols roared from both sides. As he sped for cover, he heard the marshal pounding along behind him, also trying to evade Grantree's gunmen. The marshal had a hand clapped to the side of his neck, and was angrily bellowing, "What'n hell are you sons doing? Trying to cut me down?"

"That's the risk a lawdog takes when facing killers!" Grantree called back mockingly. "Hit it again, boys!"

Another ragged volley of gunfire shredded the hush of the darkened street. Ki dove through the first shop window he came to, rolling himself into a tight ball to break the glass with his back and buttocks. Before he could extricate himself from various unknown objects, Tilden dove in and landed on his stomach.

Ki heaved the lawman off, asking, "Are you with me or after me?"

"I dunno yet," Tilden growled. "Ye gawds, what's this?"

It was a tailor's dummy. The shop, they now perceived, was the Deluxe Haberdashery and Ready-to-Wear, and when coming through the window, they'd tangled with a row of dummies draped in gentlemen's clothes. The mannequins weren't exactly of robust type or shade, but with their neat mustaches they were practically masculine.

172

"Gave me a rare turn, it did." Tilden snorted and spat. "As for you, I dunno why I don't gun you for shootin' my deputy."

"How about because I don't wear a gun?"

"I don't know anything about that. All I know is, I was making my rounds when Grantree and that attorney claimed a pack o' witnesses saw you. Then, of a sudden, those who're swearing you an' Miss Starbuck had gunned my deputy seem to be trying to gun *me*."

"You're supposed to die while arresting us. We found out that Grantree and Neville are behind the Posse Comitatus."

"It was them that killed Mastleg Thistle, wasn't it?"

"Sure. And all the rest of the miners who have been robbed and killed under that fake vigilante notice. But we've sort of blown it up in their faces, you might say. It's come down to them either pulling out or striking for the top prize, control of Virginia City."

"That's the way she lies, eh?" Tilden got to his knees and sighted his revolver on the street. "Mayhap I should deputize you."

"You don't have to. It won't scare them any or help me much. And I'm going after them anyway."

A shadow edged up against the smashed window. The marshal slung a shot at it, and it fell away. In response, a storm of gunfire broke out all around the haberdashery shop, splintering the flimsy wallboards and shattering such jagged fragments of the front window as remained attached to the frame. When it subsided, Tilden raised himself cautiously and slammed two more shots into the slackening group of muzzle flashes on the far side of the street. Somebody cursed loudly, and there was the sound of a heavy fall to the boardwalk.

Tilden crouched down and, in the lull following his shots, hastily reloaded from his cartridge belt. They could hear talking outside as curious bystanders clustered nearer. Once, during a moment of quiet, there was a faraway cry, like a scream, muffled and broken off—and Ki thought of Jessie, the huntress who perhaps had become the hunted. But mainly they heard the inquisitive gathering of drunkards, towns-folk, laborers, and river scrubs—and the persuasive baritone of Grantree, explaining that a mad killer had taken the marshal hostage.

"Yell to them," Ki demanded. "Tell them the truth!"

"To them?" Tilden scoffed. "A waste of breath. They don't have enough guts 'twixt them to blow a fart after a bean supper."

"Marshal?" Grantree called. "What're you doing in there? Come out, man, if you're still alive!" And right after that, he said in a stage voice to his growing audience of onlookers, "The marshal's obviously un-der gun, a prisoner. He's slowed with age."

Tilden lunged upright and started toward the door. Ki grabbed him by the ankle and brought him down sprawling. "Hold it!" Ki snapped. "That's what he's counting on! It's what they're all waiting for!"

Tilden struggled. "I got my job to do out there!"

"I've got one too," Ki said. "But first we have to give them something to shoot at. Here, take a dummy. I'll use this fellow."

Trundling their mannequins to the door, Ki yanked it open and threw out his, which was wearing a starched linen collar and black broadcloth. Tilden was a toss behind, with a dummy garbed in a checked suit and a derby hat. In the darkness the two figures looked like two men plunging out into the street, and they got what was waiting. A withering fusillade riddled them, and before they rolled to the boardwalk, they had become massacred merchandise.

"Disastrous! That blood-crazed murderer has killed our marshal!" Grantree bellowed. "Ain't that a hellish tragedy, though?"

"Terrible!" agreed a chorus, with a few low-pitched snickers. The men—who Ki suspected were the remaining members of the Posse—sidled forward from all quarters. Grantree scratched a match and bent close, the only one who got anywhere near a peek at the perforated dummies. In the light of his match, his expression looked flabbergasted.

And Ki and the marshal sprang outside.

Grantree jerked erect in time to have the match and his thumb blown off his hand. He swayed, groping toward a dagger whose handle had suddenly seemed to sprout from his chest, as Ki and Tilden turned their weapons on others. Then, stumbling, he fell across the dummies, cursing his final seconds alive, while his gang broke apart, startled and confused by this inexplicable attack.

"Now I know how spineless folks can be!" Tilden was raging while he fired. "I never would've believed it! Don't fret, you milksop pantywaists, you'll get what you deserve, soon's we're dead!"

The throng stood taking it, shamed and cowed as the street became a roaring funnel of gunfire. Then, for an instant, the crowd seemed to exhale a restive sigh, and Ki wondered if that might portend a change. He had seen such crowds form and alter before, as if they were living organisms. All it took was the right spark.

Running, Tilden lurched against Ki and reeled away, striving like a drunken man to keep his feet. He fetched up against the alley side of a building across from the Silverado, and put his back to it, legs braced. "Move!" he growled. "Get tending to your own job."

Ki spun around to him. "Hurt bad?"

"Slowed a mite," Tilden admitted, and blazed three rapid shots into the converging gunmen. "C'mon, vigilantes, why not lynch me!"

The gunmen staggered over their fallen comrades, and from the crowd came a quivering mutter. It was changing; Ki could feel it changing through his skin. He sensed that it was riled by what their marshal had said, but was stirred more deeply by seeing him wounded, holding off the whole killer crew. Animosity began congealing it into a mob.

A gunman snarled, "Score 'em, boys! There's only two!"

"Two, hell!" another swore. "One's hurt, t'other's unarmed!"

Then rose a new voice—a pent-up cry of yearning for a chance to scream, to rip and tear and destroy . . .

More guns joined those already blasting, but these did not send lead spanging against the alley entrance, searching for Ki and Tilden. The marshal was the first to grasp the import. "Don't tell me I put some starch in those rabbits!" His face was lined with pain, but full of triumph. "Get along with you! I got a town backin' me now, and I aim to show 'em how to burn powder!" He raised his big old .44 Dragoon. It blazed once, and somewhere a man screamed mortally.

"Pretty fair," Ki said. "See you later."

He went back down the alley, darkness cloaking him, then paused at the next street to look behind him. He had only a partial view, but it was sufficient. The Posse was beginning to scatter before a withering barrage of gunfire. But they were being engulfed by men pouring in against them, lips peeled back, eyes aflame with the crazy, killing heat of a mob. And someone had evidently ignited the Silverado's entrance torches and heaved them inside the saloon, for Ki could see a puff of lurid flame leaping from one upper corner. An instant later the street was no longer dark, but aglow with the eerie red illumination from the fire.

Tilden was right; he didn't need him.

Jessie needed him . . .

Jessie had been waiting with mounting impatience.

She'd been staying hidden behind the side of the house next door, ever since Neville arrived at his house and went inside. She might have risked sneaking closer to learn what he was doing, except that there was a guard with a rifle lounging on the porch.

176

So there she remained, chafing to act, while from the saloon district below rose echoing gunfire of increasing intensity.

She was concerned about Ki, but she couldn't leave, not without knowing more. She was seriously considering doing something, anything, guard or no, when another man came sprinting up the hill. He would have spotted her if he'd bothered to turn his head, but he ran as if possessed, through the gate in the picket fence, up the porch steps, and into Neville's house, leaving the front door open. The guard moseyed over to close it, but then, seemingly perked by curiosity, sauntered inside and shut the door behind him.

Jessie eased out from behind the corner of the neighboring house, darted across to the gate, and dove in behind some neglected shrubbery that was trying to grow along the porch. She strained to catch any sight or sound, ready to duck down the instant anyone started out the door.

For reasons known only to himself, when Neville came out, he decided not to come out the front, but to use the rear door and stroll around the side of his house. He was with the guard and the other man, and they were all staring down the dark street, trying vainly to make out how matters were going.

"Damned odd," Neville was saying. "Grantree was crowing that he'd killed those two, eh? Doesn't sound like it much. Look, Reese, you go on down there this time and find out why they're still shooting."

"Okay." Nodding, the guard balanced his rifle in the crook of his arm, and moved ahead of Neville and the other man. Then he suddenly stopped and yelled, *"Hey, boss!"*

Jessie got an instant's view of the rifle barrel swinging around to line up on her, of the other man lunging for his holster, and Neville promptly whirling and running back around the side of the house.

She triggered her pistol, which she'd already drawn as a precaution. The guard, still swinging his rifle, tottered backward and swung it high, and he went over, holding on to it like a capsizing boat with one mast. Jessie flung herself flat as the other man began defoliating the shrubbery with his gunfire. Lying prone, elbows on the ground, she took deliberate aim. The man started dodging, zigzagging backward on his toes in the haze of powdersmoke. Her shot drilled upward through his chest.

As she got up, a pistol spat down at her from a second-floor window above the porch. She sucked in her breath, scrambled up under the porch roof, thrust open the front door, and lunged inside.

The pistol lanced at her again from somewhere. It had the flat and solid crack of a short-barreled pocket pistol—a lethal weapon in close-quarters skirmishes, but difficult to train on a moving target. And Jessie was moving along the parquet hallway as fast as she could. A bullet nipped by her and hit the face of a tall grandfather clock, setting it to chiming madly.

She veered away from the clock and spotted Neville. He was on the upstairs landing, reached by a curving staircase some yards ahead, and he was sighting again, his eyes glittering above the pistol. Jessie brought up her .38 Colt and fired fast, without taking time to aim. She saw Neville back up, flinching, then turn and vanish.

She took the stairs two at a time. A door slammed shut, then quietly, furtively opened a crack when she was almost to the landing. She put a bullet through it and rushed up the rest of the steps.

Behind the door, Neville rasped furiously, "Damn you, bitch, don't try to come through! I'll kill you! I'll—" His voice broke. He was no longer an assured, coolly hard man, commanding lesser men. His streak of weakness was now laid bare, as naked as his body had been when Jessie had forced him to strip.

Naturally the door was locked. "I'm coming after you, Neville!" Jessie called, wrecking the lock with a bullet—her fifth. She only had one more left, and no time to reload. She kicked at the ruined latch, smashing the door open as Neville fired through it.

The room, evidently his bedroom, was the one over the porch. Neville was crouching by its still open window, behind a small writing desk he'd pulled aside when shooting down at her earlier.

"Put down your gun," Jessie said, and waggled her pistol. "Put it down, Neville, or I'll drop you where you stand."

She stared at him coldly, her pistol steady, straight out in front of her. There was no excitement in her now. No hurry, either. It was as if she had all the time she needed to place her single last shot, in that final split second when Chester Neville fired his pistol—

The room shook with the explosion of two shots. Jessie's spooky coolness must have shaken Neville to the core, for his bullet missed its mark, slamming into the hallway in back of her. Jessie's slug hit smack on target. Neville stiffened. The pistol in his hand wobbled, and dropped to the carpet with a soft thud. Then Neville took a quick sidestep as though he was planning to turn and walk away. Slowly, very slowly, he folded, holding both hands over his stomach, and pitched headlong out the window and struck the porch roof below.

Jessie lowered her empty weapon and advanced to the window, and as she did so, she got a glimpse of Ki, his *tanto* in his hand, standing in the bedroom door.

"Jessie! Are you—? That scream, all those shots!"

"I didn't scream," she retorted, glancing down at Neville. "I have never screamed in my entire life, as you very well know."

"Yes, of course," Ki replied with a smile, leaning to look out with her, and wondering whose scream it was that he'd heard.

Far below, they could tell that gunfire had tapered off around the blazing Silverado. But across town, a pitched battle was being fought at Flynn's Livery, where the remaining members of the Posse had been caught by the stable and corral, where most had put up their horses. Their leader had been killed, a dozen or more of their companions had been blasted into eternity, and now their tattered remnants were in frantic retreat from the swift, grim retribution descending upon them.

And just beneath Jessie and Ki sprawled Chester Neville, his malignant power in Virginia City crushed forever.

★

Chapter 17

It was late the following evening, a few hours after Mastleg Thistle's afternoon burial service. He was interred on a gentle knoll at the far south end of the Baptist cemetery, where rye grass and weeds grew among weathered, sun-bleached wooden markers, except here and there, where somebody cared enough to clear away the rank growth. Someone had left a jar of wildflowers on one grave.

From there, Jessie and Ki went to dinner, and then to visit Marshal Tilden. For once he was in his office, and would be for some time, confined to an iron cot until his injuries healed. The slash in his shoulder was not deep, and was expected to give him little trouble. The wound beneath his arm was more serious, a rib having been fractured, with a possible lung puncture. But the doctor had said he thought Tilden would survive, and Tilden knew damn well he would.

Tilden struggled up as they entered, holding his left shoulder and smiling gamely through the pain that wracked his aging frame. "Just in time, by dab. Quick, grab me that bottle before I faint."

Ki handed him the quart of whiskey that was standing on his desk, and the marshal drank deeply. Some of the color returned to his cheeks, and his voice was stronger when he asked, "Well, what d'you know?"

Jessie smiled ruefully. "Not much. Mostly we're guessing."

"Maybe we learned how the bullion was handled," Ki added.

He waited, and Tilden said, "Don't josh me. I'm sick."

Ki laughed. "All right. Obviously that much gold was a burden, and they would've had plans for disposing of it. That's why they included Enoch Balsam, who was broke, tempted, and strictly an amateur. But he had the land and the equipment, and he packed in sacks of blacksmith's coal and some bellows, and built some rock ovens at the claim site. The idea was to melt the bullion and then recast it into smaller slugs that could be divided up and carried more easily, and sold here and there inconspicuously."

"Only we surprised them before they could, right?" Tilden asked.

"Right. They held you off for four days, though, while they melted the bullion and poured it into the mine's crevices and fissures. Then they destroyed the equipment and blasted both ends of the tunnel closed, leaving the ore molded into the hill, with rubble and dirt on top of it. A hidden, manmade gold mine."

"Well, why didn't they come back before now?"

"They would have, except that their leader, Neville, was jailed for theft." Jessie didn't add that the others wouldn't have dared try to recover the loot on their own, so long as Neville had the backing of the cartel. "While in Deer Lodge, Neville met Everard—a lucky break for him, the mining expert of his gang, Balsam, having died long before. Probably Everard agreed to teach him mining for a cut of the

182

take, but then he too died. Later, when Neville needed a name for the claim lease, Everard's popped to mind."

Ki nodded. "Neville, when he got out, would have sent for his old members. That's what the torn pieces of photograph were for, a signal so they'd know it was time to regroup here, prearranged back when they took the picture off the dying Balsam. So it follows that Willie Prinzoni was a member, the piece he received having Unity on it."

"Here's where we really have to speculate," Jessie cautioned. "Those who'd know for sure are all dead now. Either Neville used the torn pieces as bait, and systematically killed the other members, or Prinzoni tried to double-cross him. Whichever it was, Neville arranged to have Prinzoni killed. The attempt failed, and Prinzoni came to us."

"That's what I call fine figurin'!" Tilden said admiringly. "Those three men from the train have been identified as San Francisco scum, so I reckon they were hunting you two after killing Prinzoni, but never even got to report to Neville. You got 'em, and Neville didn't know nothin' right at first." The marshal slapped his thigh delightedly. "So which d'you think? Was Neville killing off his gang to gain a bigger share, or was Prinzoni trying some sorta shakedown on him?"

"We think it was a shakedown," Jessie answered, "because we think Grantree was a member too. Surely they knew each other from before; their partnership formed mighty fast when Neville showed up here. Using the Silverado as an in-town listening post, and having the mine double as a hideout, they imported cheap hoodlums and outlaws to help mine the gold, and to wrest control of the area. Once Mastleg and Unity died, Neville could take over the Monteplata. And Gabe was lined up for a lynching when he got too curious about Doc Everard's claim."

"Well, mayhap we'll find the last four or five members among all the corpses." The marshal stretched sleepily on his cot. "But, 'ceptin' for details like that, it's about over, and we came out durn lucky. Oh yeah, and soon's we find out how much loot is still recoverable, you should be receivin' a plump bit o' reward."

Jessie shook her head. "See that Unity gets it, will you?"

"Sure! By ginger, woman, if I was twenty years younger..."

"I wouldn't stand a chance." Smiling, Jessie leaned over and gave Tilden's stubbly chin an affectionate pat.

Leaving the marshal's office, Ki said, "Our train doesn't depart for a while yet. Let's stop and say goodbye to Unity."

"And just happen to mention that she's in for some money?"

"If the subject comes up, Jessie, why not?"

They walked briskly to the Palace Hotel, where Ki had booked Unity a room. After the total destruction of the Silverado by fire, she'd been entirely wiped out, right down to her fiddle, and had needed a place to stay for a few days before returning to the Monteplata.

When they reached the door to Unity's room, Ki raised his hand to knock, then paused, hearing voices within. He turned and shrugged. "She's got company, Jessie."

Through the door filtered Gabe's voice: "I can't let you go it alone! I can't leave you unprotected. I've always loved you, Unity, always will!"

"Maybe we shouldn't interrupt," Jessie whispered.

Then came some feminine moans, and Unity whimpered hoarsely, "Not so fast, not so fast—but oh, oh, please, one more thrust like that!"

"Assuredly not!" Ki turned and started down the hall toward the lobby, his lips tightened in a grin.

Catching up with him in the lobby, Jessie laughed.

"Sounded like everyone was having bad timing. We'll send her a telegram from Reno."

"Ki! Oh, Ki!" a voice called out, and a second surprise in as many minutes now greeted their eyes. Francine MacNear was sashaying across the lobby, her arms outstretched. "I was hoping to bump into you. The Silverado burned down, y'know, so I'm out of a job. I've decided to return to San Francisco, and guess what? We're on the same train."

Ki linked arms with her and winked slyly at Jessie. "My, my, Francine, isn't that a coincidence?"